Memory AND Desire

LEONORA HORNBLOW

Memory AND *Desire*

April is the cruelest month, breeding
Lilacs out of the dead land, mixing
Memory and desire

RANDOM HOUSE · NEW YORK

For Ruby Schinasi

"To Carthage then I came, where a cauldron of unholy loves sang all about mine ears."

St. Augustine's *Confessions*

Memory AND Desire

CHAPTER ONE OUTSIDE it was raining. Not a driving, dramatic rain but a thin, insistent wet that seemed stuck in the air to be shaken into sudden showers that as suddenly stopped, leaving the day unchanged, the clouds and the grayness and the wet remaining.

Gordon Cram was standing at the one window in his office watching the rain fall delicately upon the pane. *Rain is not becoming to Hollywood,* he thought, *it looks abandoned, like an amusement park in the winter.*

There were puffy, soiled clouds in a blind sky, a sky darker than the street, so that it was like a photograph of itself held upside down. He knew the short, uninteresting street so well that he saw it without looking at it, parking lot at one end, Frank's Drugstore at the other, and, in the middle, the East Gate of the R.A.M. Studios and the shoebox of a shelter for the studio police. As Gordon looked out a policeman came from the shelter and spoke to a small group of people who then reluctantly moved along and out of Gordon's sight. They were part of a band of autograph seekers who gathered every afternoon to watch the actors drive out of the studio.

Nor rain, nor snow, thought Gordon, *and on a lousy day like this, the lunatics.*

After scanning the sky the policeman returned to his shelter. A car drove quickly through the gate, sending a puddle of water into the air. A few of the fans reappeared, and Gordon heard them calling and waving at the car.

Must be Bobby Duncan, Gordon thought, *who else would own a scarlet car?*

A single, sodden leaf tapped against the glass. Gordon tapped back with his fingernail and yawned. This sort of weather made him sleepy. He wanted a day with the wind blowing and the sky a hard, sunny cobalt, a cold, clear day at the beach, white waves breaking and curling, breaking and curling on sand. He had been thinking about such a day at odd moments for a month. It had begun when the rains began the first week in April and now April was almost over.

Will I ever get out of here? he asked himself with the restlessness that a sense of the passing of time always gave him. He thought again, as he had been thinking intermittently since it had arrived, of the letter from the editor of *Holiday* which offered him a free summer in Europe if he would do a series of articles for them.

If I could finish this job, get it right, get it set, so that Henry won't have any trouble when they start shooting, if I could do that by June, then I could make it . . . England first, do a couple from London . . . then

France, Venice for at least two weeks, maybe a look at Spain, and back in New York by October. I like New York in October.

The old, ugly palm trees that bordered the street blew in the rising wind and made a soughing, sad sound that came to Gordon through the window.

He turned from the view of the dull street, now excited by his plans and trying to put them out of his mind. He was having trouble with the script and couldn't cure that by making timetables into the future.

He sat down at the tidy desk, disliking the tidiness. If he had been working well the glass top would have been churning with notes and papers and cardboard folders. Twisting a paper clip, he tried to turn his mind to the scene he had been writing.

In Gordon's opinion writing for the screen was a well paid, mildly interesting thing to do if you didn't have to do it all the time. He did not see it as the gilt-edged trap that some of his colleagues did, blaming their unwritten works on the temptations of the movie industry. Listening to their laments Gordon often thought, *At these prices you can afford a neurosis.* Personally, he felt that writing for the movies wasn't writing at all. It was a confection of scenes and situations beaten into final shape with two other men who carried pencils as well as their titles "producer" and "director."

Gordon's office was on the third, or writers' floor of the Administration Building at R.A.M. Studios. It was known as the New Building although it had been built fifteen years ago, a looming, squat, white structure unadorned as an egg. Gordon called it "the air-conditioned nightmare."

His office was exactly like every other on the third floor; biscuit-colored walls, glass-topped desk, leather couch, two uncomfortable chairs and a lean metal table on wheels which held the typewriter. All he had brought of his own was a big, round, glass ash tray and the alarm clock.

Every year for the past twelve (except three he had spent in the army) Gordon had come to Hollywood, occupied an identical office and received increasing sums of money for writing screenplays. This took anywhere from eight weeks to six months because, even though he wrote dialogue with ease, progress wasn't always as smooth as he planned.

Like this one, he thought, *we're stuck on this one.*

He looked at the clock now—4:30. He worked, in New York or Hollywood or wherever, from nine in the morning until six at night with a full hour for lunch. When he first began to write for his living, having walked out on the job for his father, he had arbitrarily set those hours, partly to show his father, who had snorted, "Writers, I know writers, sleep all day, sit up all night picking at a machine, call *that* work, ha!"

Gordon pulled a sheet of paper from the typewriter and, not looking, added it to the pile on the desk. He rubbed his fist into his eyes, wondering if the rain could be the reason his head ached. *Or maybe I need glasses.*

He pressed the buzzer and Miss Sawyer came in.

"What's doing in the great world?" he asked.

"No mail, no messages except Mr. Calder to remind you dinner at 7:30," she paused, "and he asked would you please pick up Mrs. Tavis."

"Sure," Gordon said.

He scribbled *Alma Tavis* on a memo pad. Marjorie Sawyer's voice had an artificial tone. Had she heard rumors—if there were rumors—foolish of Henry to leave such a message. Perhaps Henry didn't know. Perhaps he did. Gordon would like to have been able to ask him but he knew that he wouldn't. He rarely discussed his personal affairs even with those directly concerned and sometimes not even with them. When people confided in him, which they often did, it always struck him as strange that they revealed private matters; but he listened. He was an excellent listener.

"My father never had a friend that I can remember. I can still hear him, 'Don't talk to people, none of their business what we do.' "

Gordon had said this to Alma Tavis one night when she had complained that he told her nothing about himself. "You sit and listen and don't say anything," she had laughed, "you'd make an ideal analyst."

"I'd love to have you on my couch."

"No, be serious, you never do talk about yourself."

"Aren't there better topics, Mrs. Tavis? Let's choose a topic."

"At least," Alma had sighed, "you're not one of the fiends who won't talk to women. You just won't talk to anyone."

Again Marjorie's voice interrupted his reverie, "Go any better today?"

"Not much." He picked up a batch of blue pages crisscrossed with penciled changes and gave them to her.

"Marge, will you find out who the Calders' eye doctor is and make an appointment for me?"

"Eyes bothering you?"

"A little," he said, "or maybe I'm just tired of being the only writer around who doesn't wear horn-rimmed glasses."

"You'll be photographed against that wall of books next."

"And smoking a pipe," Gordon smiled.

"No, that's for actors." Marjorie smiled and waited for instructions.

The light began to fade in the way that it does in California. Soon it would be dark with no twilight interval.

"There ought to be a new word for this time of day out here," Marjorie said.

"What about depressing," Gordon suggested.

He thought of the lingering dusk in New York when the day ended and night had not yet begun; the lights came on, long vertical ribbons in the office buildings, patchwork patterns in the apartment houses, the sky turning violet across Central Park, the silhouette of the city set in gilt and silver illuminating the hour, the ineluctable hour when New York becomes the city in the dream, beckoning and promising and magical.

Gordon felt the quicksand tug of nostalgia; he thought of the streets of the city, the feel of pavement beneath the foot and beneath the pavement the raw, substantial rock that New York was built upon. The constant, seething movement of buses and taxicabs, of boats and barges on the two rivers and of the people walking in the way that people walk in New York as if they had some place to go and were on their way and in a hurry. And the air, the irascible, alive, tainted air—to Gordon, among others, nourishing and necessary and beloved.

8

But all that he said was, "I miss New York a lot."

"You'll have been here four months next week," Marjorie said.

"Looks as if I'll be here four more." Gordon put a dust cover on his typewriter. "God help any writer on a romance being tailored to fit an aging 'first lady of the screen.' How did I ever get into this mess in the first place?"

"Mr. Calder always hollers for you when he's in trouble, and 'Rim of Heaven' was trouble. Shall I send for coffee?"

"No, let's take the rest of the afternoon off."

"Want to take anything home?" she asked.

He shook his head. "See you tomorrow, Marge."

"Don't forget, seven-thirty at the Calders," she said. "Have fun."

Gordon lit a cigarette. For the last seven years, whenever he was working in Hollywood, Marjorie Sawyer had been his secretary. He picked up the slip of paper on which he had written Alma Tavis and tore it in two. He wasn't fooling Marjorie. She knew.

He went back to the window. The sign of Frank's Drugstore had been turned on, and the red neon letters shone unreal and somehow sinister in the failing light. The rain had stopped.

2

Lying on the sofa in his office, Henry Calder was eating an apple and reading for the second time the sequences that Gordon had turned in the day before.

9

He finished the apple and his reading at the same time; then, taking careful aim, he threw the core across the room at the wastebasket.

Sitting up, he clipped the pages together and placed them in a handsome black binder which bore on its front in large golden letters the legend MR. CALDER'S SCRIPT. "Doesn't sound like Gordon," he said aloud, frowning.

He took off his glasses and polished them on his trouser leg. His face wore an expression of concern. Until a few days ago he had felt unlimited confidence in Gordon's ability; he had known him for many years and this would be the seventh picture that they had worked on together. Henry had often said that he would be a happy man without needing to give more than an occasional thought to his occupational ulcer if all the writers he worked with were as dependable as Cram.

But it had to be admitted that to date this script was discouraging. Somehow it was not shaping, not settling, and something about Gordon himself caused Henry particular disquiet.

He crossed the width of the wide room over a carpet the color and texture of moss to the broad plain table of wood, bleached beige, that he used as a desk.

He flipped a switch. "Rhea, see if Mr. Cram can come in."

He drew an arrow on his immaculate blotter, thinking of things to say to Gordon. He must be careful not to be too discouraging. Cram was sure of himself and his talent, but like all writers he needed encouragement and reassurance. "Not all the hams are actors," Henry mused as he waited.

Rhea replied through the speaker, "Mr. Cram just left the lot for the day. Shall I try him at the hotel?"

"Never mind, I'll see him tonight. And remind me to call him as soon as I get in tomorrow morning. I can probably go over this with him before I see the wardrobe tests."

"Okay, and they're ready with the rushes whenever you are."

"Be right there. Let Mr. Altman know, maybe he'd like to run with me."

It was nearly dark outside. Henry saw through the big window that the sky was the color of silver long unpolished. He wished suddenly that he, too, could leave the studio and go home.

It was curious of Gordon to leave so early. In all the years that Henry had known him he couldn't remember his ever having stopped work before six.

"Will you get Mrs. Calder, Rhea?" he asked.

His thoughts remained on Gordon as he drew feathers on the arrow. "Maybe it isn't Alma Tavis, maybe it's his wife. She's an odd woman for Gordon, but they've been married for years."

When Henry first met Gordon he was married and, Henry had thought, unhappily. At first, not even Sue knew why the Crams stayed married—neither of them was Catholic. It was later that they had found out about the child.

"Mrs. Calder is not at home," said Rhea's disembodied voice, "she can't be reached because she's at a Parent-Teachers' meeting at the school. Any message?"

"Only one of deepest sympathy," said Henry.

He recalled now that Sue had been grumbling about

the meeting last night. Henry reached for another apple; there were a dozen in the pottery bowl. Sue sent especially to a ranch in Oregon for them.

He wondered whether he should talk to Gordon, attempt to find out what was bothering him. But, as he had learned, Gordon was hard to talk to about personal things, though he was an easy and agreeable person to be with. "Anyway," Henry said aloud, "that's for Sue, those heart-to-heart talks."

"They're ready in Room D," came from the speaker. "Mr. Altman will join you there."

"On my way," he said. Dismissing Gordon Cram from his mind, he walked out of his office and down the corridor to the elevators.

3

GORDON drove along Hollywood Boulevard thinking how inexpressibly, exasperatingly ugly it was. Before he had first seen it twelve years ago he had expected a cross between the tropical playground of a travel folder and a chromium-plated county fair. Instead he had found it garish and cheap with the taste and smell of gritty dust.

"The Hollywood Chamber of Commerce does a hell of a job," Gordon had then said, peering out of the car window. "Where's that paradise they advertise?"

The man in the seersucker suit from the studio publicity department who had been sent to meet Gordon hadn't understood. "Now about Hollywood Boulevard," he had explained, "it's not the best part of town, not

12

residential, you know. Fact is, it looks a little like Broadway with the lights and everything."

"Broadway can afford to look that way," Gordon had said severely. "It's Broadway."

He never overcame this first impression of dismal mediocrity. And it now occurred to him and not for the first time that what he most disliked about Hollywood had singularly little to do with his work or the people who employed him.

In spite of his pleasant and profitable Hollywood record, when Gordon got on the train at the end of a stay, the script stamped "Final Complete" in his suitcase, he was sorry for those who stayed behind, whether from choice or necessity. Seeing the buff-colored Pasadena station recede always gave him a moment of positive elation and soon he would be thinking about a new novel or short story or an idea for the play he intended to write one day.

He concluded that he was in the enviable position of being able to limit his dislike of Hollywood (to use a generic term for the sprawling settlements from Los Angeles to Santa Monica) to the smog-bound climate, the dreary local newspapers and the curious circumstance that no single corner of it resembled a true city. San Francisco with its handsome face could indeed afford to look askance at its southern neighbor that had no face at all.

Gordon Cram would be thirty-eight years old on his next birthday. He looked younger than that, perhaps, for one reason, because his hair was cropped short. He was not handsome nor was he ugly, though at various times women had thought that he was both. He looked

13

sunburned, thanks in part to a portable sun lamp which he used daily, not out of vanity, but out of a conviction that it protected him from the common cold. In his narrow brown face, his light-colored eyes looked like marbles; even when the rest of his face was in repose they regarded the world with a lively, encompassing glance. There was a determined, controlled expression around his mouth that disappeared when he smiled, a sudden, spontaneous smile usually followed by his loud, easy laughter.

There was something about the way he walked, drove a car, inhaled a cigarette, that conveyed the strong, sure sense that he was a man whom women liked, who knew about them, who had the capacity to deal with them, to comfort them as well as bring them unhappiness.

Gordon was an uncommonly healthy man. The only day of his life that he had ever spent entirely in bed had been with a girl called Laura Davis in a hotel in Newark just before he had enlisted in the army. He often thought of that day and wondered what had become of Laura—she'd been such a pretty girl.

He slowed down the car and bought the evening papers from the dwarf who had sold them on that corner of Hollywood Boulevard for years. He scanned the headlines and dropped the papers on the seat beside him. One of the main differences between New York and Hollywood was in the newspapers, he thought. It was a difference in attitude. Most New Yorkers were pleasantly pathological about newsprint. Even his father, who had so mistrusted the written word and scorned those who wrote, had read his newspapers from first page

14

to last, folding them and seaming them, so that he read them virtually inch by inch.

In New York Gordon's day was timed by the newspapers; around midnight he'd go out to get the early edition of the next morning's paper; others were delivered at his door at dawn and he picked them up before he ate breakfast and at this time of the evening he'd buy the evening papers, all of them. When he opened the door of his apartment Louise would inevitably call, "Gordon, is that you, did you bring the papers?"

Gordon stayed at the Bel Vista Hotel on Sunset Boulevard in Beverly Hills, twenty-five minutes from the R.A.M. Studios and five minutes from Alma Tavis' house.

At the desk in the lobby he collected his mail and room key. On the bill his room was described as a bed-sitting room combination. When Gordon had lived at the Bel Vista before the war it had been a half vacant, pseudo-Spanish eyesore, but with wartime profits the entire building had been remodeled into an amorphous style known as contemporary.

Gordon's room had chocolate-brown walls and built-in furniture. The twin beds were set together in an alcove and covered with rough persimmon-colored material. It resembled a room in a department store's "Home of Tomorrow," even to the lacquer-framed print of Picasso's "Harlequin" that hung over the desk. Gordon missed the impersonal, homely furniture that hotel bedrooms used to have and the walls painted the white of French vanilla ice cream; then you knew where you were.

He had lived a great deal in hotels and his response to them was always the same: he loved them at first, everything about them, the bare closets, the sample-size soap, the paper and post cards and yellow telegraph blanks in the desk drawer. The room empty of memory and association was implicit with adventure to him: he would have a sense that something was about to happen, something fine and unexpected; he'd unpack everything, lean out of the window to see what he could of the unaccustomed view, order a sandwich from room service, the newspapers from the newsstand, and he'd be established, more at home in those first minutes in the new hotel room than he would be anywhere on earth.

But after a few days the feeling would disappear, he would be aware that the place had a smell until then unnoticed, he'd identify the odor and find it repugnant (the room in the Bel Vista now smelled to him unmistakably of old hairbrushes); overwhelmingly and illogically he would want to move.

In the three months that he had occupied it Gordon had added little to Room 119 in the Bel Vista. There were the books he managed to accumulate wherever he stayed and the New York papers and magazines scattered around. On the desk was his portable typewriter and a block of the light-blue typing paper he liked and a dozen sharpened pencils stuck in a water tumbler. On the dresser there were two cartons of Chesterfields, a box of long wooden kitchen matches and a bottle of Scotch. By the bed was a clock in a leather traveling case that his wife had given him for Christmas and one of the two big glass ash trays that he always took on his travels along with the small sun lamp and the typewriter. Nothing that could not be packed into his suitcase.

He glanced at the envelopes that he had waited to

16

examine. There were two bills, an advertisement and a letter from his wife in the white envelope with her name and address printed on its back in neat dark-blue type, ordinary note paper obtainable at any stationery store. Louise had used it ever since he had known her.

He sat down on one of the beds in the alcove and read the letter, a page and a half single-spaced on the typewriter. Louise's letters were succinct, full of news of people they knew together, of her job (she was an editor for Dover House) and questions about his script. As Gordon read the letter over it seemed to him to contain friendship and affection and no hint of recrimination. He could almost hear her quiet voice. He realized and, as always with relief, that she made no mention of what he had come to think of as the trouble between them. But as they rarely spoke of it when they were together there seemed little reason to write about it when they were apart. In the last few years Louise discussed it hardly at all and only on a night when she couldn't sleep, when the memory plagued her and she had to talk about it and she would talk about it only with him. For one thing, very few other people knew, or even suspected.

How remarkable that in twelve years so few people had found out about the child! No one knew except those who had known at the beginning. *If we had been living out here, it would have been impossible,* Gordon thought. *If you have something to hide, such as a child born an idiot, live in a big city.* Then he felt the mixture of guilt and revulsion that always accompanied his thoughts about the thing.

Unconsciously he sighed as he replaced the letter in

17

the envelope. There were times when he found himself missing Louise and this was one of them. He wished that he could talk to her, tell her about the script, say, "I'm stuck, Louise." And she would help, she had never failed to help. What a bright girl she was and how strange that he thought of her so affectionately, yet not for a single second in the way that would change her from a miserable woman to a happy one.

He went to the bureau, opened the bottle of Scotch and made himself a drink, wishing that he had ordered some ice.

"I'll never be able to figure it out," he said to himself, putting the cap back on the soda, "how you can totally stop wanting to sleep with someone you loved and keep on wanting to sleep with someone you don't even like. That dancer, La Flamme, for instance—what a tiresome bitch and the girl called Page and Ellen Post—Ellen was the worst possible bore except in bed. Clearly one thing has very little to do with the other, but it's wonderful when you get both. In the beginning with Louise it was like that. . . ."

But he didn't want to think about all that at the end of a stale, unproductive day.

He picked up the telephone.

"Order, please," said the operator.

He gave her Alma Tavis' number.

Gordon loosened his tie, placed the pillows from both beds behind his back and, drinking his drink slowly, he waited for the telephone to ring.

CHAPTER TWO

THE TELEPHONE
at Alma Tavis' house was on an exceedingly long cord
which reached into every room. Alma carried it about
with her when she was at home, disentangling it from
the furniture legs and defying death at least once a day
by answering it when she was in the bathtub. The telephone was painted the same chalky pale green that was
the dominant color of the decoration of the house. Pale
green did not accurately describe it; it was pale green as
a leaf of baby lettuce is pale green or the tight bud of
a white rose. Alma loved the color and used it for many
things, the painted walls of the rooms, nightgowns and
note paper and the crepe-de-chine sheets on her bed and
the telephone.

Alma and the telephone were now in the tiny mir-
rored hall between the bathroom and the bedroom. The
mirrors were closet doors. Between two of them there
was a high, small window and beneath it a table was
installed which exactly fitted the space, a workman-like

table which held a magnifying mirror as well as an assortment of jars, bottles, tubes, boxes, pots of every kind of cream, powder, oil, unguents, pastes, pomades and cosmetics, all arranged in meticulous rows.

Alma sat in front of the table looking quite unlike herself. Her hair was wrapped in a linen towel, her features blanked out with thick cold cream. In her hand she held a small rubber mallet which she first dipped into a bowl of ice, then hit herself with it hard in the face. Over the beautifully cut bones the cruel, cold mallet struck for four minutes by the clock.

She glanced at the clock to time herself: nearly 5:15. It would be at least another hour before she could expect Gordon's call, but about this time every evening she began waiting for it. She had met him less than three months ago and already their life together had formed its own design.

For no reason that was clear to her she sighed. It sounded wistful and she was not. Since Gordon's entrance into her life she had determined to be happy with him, for she knew her time with him was measured. That would be one of the penalties.

The four minutes were over. She moistened a square of cotton wool with a stinging liquid and removed the cream. The skin beneath was as fresh and flawless as a child's. She then spread a dark clay over her face, regarding the clock again. It was essential if the mask was to be effective that it remain for twenty minutes and that she did not speak while it was on and drying.

Even in Hollywood, which is well known for its abundance of pretty women, Alma Tavis was admired and acknowledged not just as another pretty girl, but as a beauty, a beauty in the grand tradition. She was so lovely that she had become a legend even in these realistic times.

Alma was thirty-one years old. She had been beautiful all of her life; for the last fifteen years she had been working at it. As she applied the clay, she thought that for the last five she had been working hard at it.

The telephone emitted a warning purr; then it rang. She picked it up, holding it a little away from her ear.

"Crestview 6-8101?" a woman's voice inquired. "I have a call for you. Go ahead." There was a clicking sound.

"Mrs. Tavis," he said.

"Hello, darling," she said, surprised and trying hard not to move her lips. "You're very early."

"You all right?" he asked. "You sound funny?"

"I'm fine," she said, feeling the clay tighten and pull at her cheeks. "I've got some stuff on my face."

She liked the sound of his laughter, loud and close in her ear. She held the telephone tight.

"I'm glad you're early," she said.

A soft silence ensued which Gordon broke. "Something odd happened today."

"What, darling?" Alma asked.

"Henry left a message with my secretary for me to pick you up tonight."

"What's odd about that?"

"I thought that we wanted to be reasonably discreet," Gordon said.

"Oh."

Gordon asked: "Did you tell Sue Calder about us?"

"I didn't have to," Alma said, the mask splitting and splintering as she spoke. "She knew."

There was another silence. Then his voice sounded far away: "Hold on a second, will you," he said, "I'm trying to light a cigarette."

It seemed a long while that she sat there holding on to the telephone, her happy feeling ebbing. A woman alone in a hall of mirrors, waiting for a voice and not knowing whether it would be loving or curt. There was something horridly familiar about it. She stared at the eyebrow pencils on the table, reading over and over the two words: Dark brown, dark brown, dark brown.

Then the voice: "What time are we due?"

"We were asked for seven-thirty."

"Means eight."

"You are always so prompt," Alma said, "Sue counts on you."

"You've corrupted me," he said. "Will you come here or shall I come over?"

"I don't think so," she said.

"What's the matter?" he said.

"Why don't you take a nap? I've got a lot of ground work to do."

"Ground work?"

"A facial." She felt herself relenting a little, "Why don't we leave early instead?"

"Um-mm," he said.

"Unless you are afraid it will cause talk," she added, making a face at herself in the mirror.

She heard him draw in his breath. She waited.

"Tell Ivy to go home. I'll be there in fifteen minutes."

"But. . . ."

"Don't worry about your dress. I'll zip the zipper."

"Hooks and eyes," Alma said.

"What?"

"Hooks and eyes," she repeated, "on my dress."

"I can handle them."

"Come right now."

"I'm going to take a shower."

"No, now," Alma demanded. "Now, this minute." The long desolate moment was forgotten, "You can take a shower here."

"All right," he said.

"Darling," she said. "Hurry up, darling. . . ."

2

WHEN one met Alma for the first time the inevitable question was: "Why isn't she in pictures?" "The answer is simple," Alma would say, "I have no talent. Most women secretly believe that they are born actresses. I have proof that I am not." Alma would laugh telling it, "Ray Tavis directed my test, everybody did everything they could to help me, Bob Duncan was in it, Martha Stanton coached me and I was awful. I ran out of the projection room and hid in the ladies' room for an hour. I made Ray swear he'd destroy it with his own hands—and he did!"

Alma might never have come to Hollywood at all if Ray Tavis had not seen her on one of his visits to New York. He had been at the Stork Club playing Russian Bank (he refused to play gin-rummy since it had become popular). He had looked up from his cards across the room and asked, "Who is that one?"

At that time, seven years ago, Alma Fletcher was the most photographed girl in New York. She posed for beer advertisements and cold cream and sterling silver and cigarettes. Her face was displayed on posters and billboards and magazine covers. She looked almost as beautiful in them as she really was.

Harry Durand, Ray's agent, was pleased that he had asked about a girl, any girl. For the past several days Harry had been having a difficult time with Ray, who had announced that he was through with women. Tavis was Durand's most important client. Harry believed in few things but one of them was a seven-year contract with no options. Ray Tavis had this kind of a contract with R.A.M. Studios. He was an Austrian and one of the best paid of all the picture directors and this entitled him to unlimited demands on Harry Durand's time and ingenuity. "Ray needs a lot of handling," he would say, "and you gotta keep a client happy."

But Ray Tavis was not happy. He had just ended another in a series of much-publicized and occasionally bizarre romances, this time with a young actress, Sherry Laine, whose career he had somewhat assisted. Aside from her manifest attractions, Miss Laine possessed a quick temper and an unerring aim when throwing small objects. "The breakage," Ray said, "had been excessive."

"How can you leave her?" Harry Durand had asked Ray. "Every man in America would like to be in your shoes."

"My shoes have nothing to do with it," Ray had

answered. "She bores me. I finish this picture and I go to New York."

He finished the picture. He went to New York. Sherry Laine married her cameraman the weekend after in Las Vegas. Ray was furious and disconsolate. He forgot her bad temper and her lack of conversation. He remembered only the things about her which it is not wise for a man to remember about a woman who has married another man. After sulking for several nights he allowed Harry to persuade him to go to the Stork Club and at the other end of the room was Alma Fletcher. At first Ray could see only her profile and then she turned her head and he saw her face.

"I would care to meet her," he said.

The following afternoon at five o'clock Harry Durand appeared at Ray's suite at the Plaza with Alma. How he managed to meet her and produce her in less than twenty-four hours was an agent's secret.

When they came in Ray was sitting on the sofa surrounded by photographs. "Peoples' disgusting daughters," he complained, "agents' hideous clients. Miss Fletcher, I am glad to see your beautiful face."

Alma smiled. She was accustomed to people telling her she was beautiful, but the way Ray Tavis said it made her vaguely uncomfortable.

"Come sit by the window," he said.

"Oh, how wonderful!" Alma exclaimed, looking out at Central Park in the snow.

"Isn't it?" Ray said as proudly as if he had planted it. "I stay at this hotel for the view, also because it is old and looks old. In Hollywood I get lonely to see something old, everything out there is so new, don't you think?"

"I've never been there," Alma said.

"We will arrange that. But first tell me what you will drink."

He was drinking a martini of his own making, a martini so dry and delicate that it was almost invisible in the glass.

On the console table was a small traveling bar, bottles and equipment, all standing tidily in a monogrammed pigskin case.

"I don't know," Alma said. She was tired. She had worked all day and was unhappy without knowing why. She wondered to herself rather wearily what she was doing there.

There was something about Ray Tavis, too, that made her feel strange and shy. She looked at his narrow, dark face with the thin, bitter mouth.

"I am a gifted bartender. Isn't that true, Harry?" he demanded.

"The best," Harry said. "I'm telling you, Miss Fletcher, he's terrific, dear."

"Well, I like frozen daiquiris," said Alma.

"In February. Oh, my God," Ray said. "Try this."

He gave her his martini.

He waited.

"I can't taste it," Alma said politely, "I like sweet drinks."

"So do I, sometimes," Ray said. "That is why I drink ice-cream soda."

He poured the pale martini mixture into a cold glass. "Try another."

Alma drank three martinis, one after another, with no visible effect. Ray was entranced.

"I do not like women who cannot drink," he declared. "Now we can fall in love."

Alma noticed that Harry Durand had disappeared between the second and the third martini.

"But first . . ." Ray leaned over her chair.

Alma was startled. She thought he would be more subtle.

He worked at the clasp of the heavy gold chain she was wearing at her throat.

"You must never wear a necklace," he said firmly. "Nothing to distract from that face."

He unfastened the necklace. "Promise me that you will throw it out."

"Why?"

"I have told you why." He took her hand. "I am going to buy you a present if you promise never to wear it."

"What?" Alma asked, wondering.

"A tourmaline," he replied, "the color of your eyes, smoky green."

"I've never seen a tourmaline."

"You shall. Now take off those bracelets," he continued, "you are too beautiful to go clink-clank like those other girls."

Alma laughed.

"And now we will go to the Colony and have our dinner."

At the Colony they asked each other questions. Alma told Ray that she was twenty-six years old, that she came from a town he had never heard of called Kensington, Ohio, that Prier, the famous photographer, had discov-

27

ered her and made her the most highly paid and sought-after model in New York, that her family was pleased by her success but her mother wished that she would fall in love and marry and settle down.

"In America do they all mean the same thing?" Ray had wanted to know.

Ray Tavis had been born in Austria, he explained to Alma, a member of a small, dull family. "They wanted me to be a musician—so boring. It was also absurd—I did not have the patience and, I tell you this in confidence, I also didn't have the ability. So I ran away to Munich where I had a school friend."

He had done many odd things before he drifted, quite by chance, into the studio of a motion-picture company in Vienna. The films immediately fascinated him and he set out to observe and learn everything that he could. When his instinct and his knowledge began to blend, he went to Berlin and directed his first picture.

Then later he went to Paris where he made the pictures that were to secure his success and which brought him to the attention of Hollywood. In Paris he married and bought an apartment on the rue du Bac and had all his books bound in scarlet calf.

In time he had received an offer from Hollywood which was too tempting to refuse. He also wanted to see how they made pictures in the United States, but he did not expect to stay long. His wife would not come with him because she considered anyone who would leave Paris for Hollywood an imbecile.

"So now I have no wife," Ray said. "But I have stayed so long I am a citizen and I own a house on the Pacific Palisades. Some people compare it to the south of

28

France. Maybe it is, if you don't look at the drive-ins and the motels and the grass which is not green."

When she returned to the apartment she shared with her cousin Phyllis, Alma awakened her.

"What's the matter, no screen test?" Phyllis had said, and yawned.

"I had a simply wonderful time."

"What's he like?"

"Not like anyone we know," Alma had answered. "Bossy and foreign."

"Is he good-looking?"

"Not a bit." Alma had shivered, pulling the pins out of her long hair. "He's nervous and thin and graceful, too, like a snake."

"Like a snake," Phyllis echoed. "How divine! Can't wait to meet him, ugh!"

Alma began to brush her hair.

"Well?"

"Well, he has deep-set eyes that look right at you and he sounds like Charles Boyer."

"Now you're talking," Phyllis said, sitting up in bed. "Did he ask for another date?"

"Dinner tomorrow night."

"A pass?"

"No pass."

"You like him?"

"I'm not sure, Phyl."

"There's always so much about him in the columns, that's all I mean, Alma."

Alma sat at the foot of Phyllis' bed. "He's going to buy me a tourmaline. He says they match my eyes."

"Too bad your eyes don't match emeralds."

29

Phyllis watched the brush move against the silky strands of hair, thinking that everything about Alma had a romantic quality. Her hair, for instance, that on any other head would be called light brown was on Alma, even in Kensington, Ohio, called dark gold.

"Go back to sleep, Phyl," Alma said as she went into the bathroom.

"Alma, honey," Phyllis called after a moment.

"Yes?"

"Take care."

Alma laughed. "Don't worry about little Alma Fletcher."

Six weeks later Ray Tavis asked her to marry him. She wasn't in love with Ray any more than she had been with the other men she had known since she was fourteen years old. It puzzled and perturbed her that she had never once even thought that she was in love but she kept hoping that it would happen; after all, it happened to everyone. She had read about it and heard about it and she waited. But she wasn't in love with Ray. Perhaps if she married him she would fall in love with him afterwards; that was the way it had been with Doris Haley, her best friend in Kensington.

She liked Ray, she liked him better than anyone else; he intrigued her—she had never known anyone like him. He talked to her about everything on earth, for he knew a lot about an astounding number of things. He gave her books to read and music to listen to and took her with him to look at the paintings in the galleries on Fifty-seventh Street. As Mrs. Tavis she would have an enviable life, she thought; he was famous and successful and rich. Those were the things she had wanted to attain —that was why she had left Ohio. She was tired of New York; she had gone as far as she could go as a model. She wanted another kind of existence. She wanted a home and a husband and Ray was eminently eligible, everyone said so, everyone thought she would be a fool to let him go.

Ray Tavis wanted to marry her for a variety of reasons. For one, he decided that he ought to be married: he was bored with the disorganized way he had been conducting his life, tired of the course of his previous affairs, the end implicit in the beginning. And most of all he was tired of actresses and their preoccupation with themselves. He had to work with them, that was enough. Alma wanted no career, she would be his beautiful wife, coveted by other men. He could give her the sort of life that he felt sure she wanted. He found her delightful to be with, malleable to his moods; against his consuming nervous energy she was tranquil, undemanding and exquisite to look upon. Ray knew that she was not in love with him but he did not put too high a premium on love; many women had loved him and always it had ended in scenes and emotional hangovers. Alma would bring him nothing but her gentleness, her kindness; he knew that he could depend on her for that. But that she seemed not to be attracted to him did concern him; Alma's absence of ardor made him curious, for he had discerned that aside ·from the essential sweetness of her nature she must have a capacity for love. Beneath what he described in his thoughts as her not-wantingness he felt that there would be a passionate woman.

"When we are married and she has appeased her

middle-class morality she will be ready to learn about love," he told himself.

In the six weeks that he had known her Ray was aware how much he had influenced her. The way she dressed and moved, even in her manner of speech, she was beginning to reflect his taste and his style. If he could accomplish that, surely the rest would follow. "I have had no failures yet," he reassured himself.

"Many Anglo-Saxon women are not really cold," he had said to Alma. "They are just sleeping beauties."

"Do they never wake up?" Alma asked.

"That depends on the man."

"But you should have an already awakened wife—not take a chance on the unknown."

"I am an explorer," he said.

They were married three days later.

Ray and Alma had one abiding interest together and that was Alma Fletcher Tavis. For the first months of their marriage they worked unceasingly and agreeably upon this project.

It was Ray who decided that pale, pale green should be "her color." And Ray who said that she should not wear a mink coat, though to Alma, as to many young women, this was a symbol of achievement. "We will buy a mink coat," Ray had said, "and use it to line a black coat. It will be more chic."

And one perfume that would be "her perfume" just as the green was "her color." When the perfume had been selected, a pervasive mixture of rose and jasmine and ambergris, it was ordered in plain quart jugs directly from the maker in Paris so that Alma would use it generously. Among Ray's often expressed dislikes were women who used a little perfume. "Fah," he would say in great pain, "those few drops behind the ear, what good do they think that will do?"

The interior of her closets was lacquered with the scent and her drawers lined with flannel that had been soaked overnight in the perfume and silken sachets were fastened to every dress.

There was the decoration of her bedroom for them to consider and the room adjoining, which Ray called her "boudoir," a word that Alma found entrancingly old-fashioned.

Then there were things to collect, to search for in shops, ornaments of white jade and white coral and blanc de chine and crystal, but not silver. "Silver is so expected," said Ray.

A hairdresser came to their house every other day who brushed and arranged Alma's hair in new styles to amuse Ray. Altogether the time passed swiftly if idly, and Alma, beautiful in the beautiful dresses in the beautiful rooms, posed in a series of tableaux. It would probably have taken quite a while before she tired of this, but Ray tired first.

Alma liked Hollywood. Everyone was kind to her, everyone admired her but when Ray was at the studio she was lonely and missed her cousin Phyllis and the other girls who had been models at the same agency in New York.

It was at about this time that Ray said, "Henry Calder is back and tomorrow night I take you to meet him."

"Who is he?" Alma asked.

"He's a producer at the studio," Ray told her. "Before

he was married I saw him a lot, since not so much but now that I, too, have a wife we will be more together."

"What is his wife like?" Alma asked.

"She is too fresh. I do not care for her," Ray had answered.

"Is she pretty?"

"To some she is, to me she isn't," Ray answered, "but she behaves as if she was."

The next night they went to dine at the Calders and Alma liked them immediately, but there was something about them that made her doubtful of her life with Ray. The Calders seemed so complete, so content.

Alma said to Ray on their way home, "I think they're dear. I hope we see a lot of them."

"That is good."

"Do you think they liked me?"

"Sue told me that Helen of Troy must have looked like you."

Alma and Sue became friends. On the nurse's day out Alma would go to the Calders and help Sue take care of her little boys. Those afternoons pushing the baby in his pram, going into the village to shop, were like the old, easy days in Kensington.

In many ways Alma was happy in her marriage, except for one thing which she knew was profoundly disturbing to Ray. He had to admit that she was still a sleeping beauty. "You should see a doctor," he'd said, discouraged. "There is something wrong with you. You are not like other women."

Alma supposed he must be right. He had had so much experience with women, and since the age of fourteen she had realized that she was not the same as most girls

34

she knew in her attitude toward men. For one thing she had no curiosity; what the girl whispered and giggled about seemed to her to be far from fun. She had moments of being distressed about it but most of the time she was uninterested. She couldn't understand it. Many times she had liked a boy until he began his exploratory love-making. She remembered the summer nights when she was young in Kensington, the sticky, lingering kisses on the dark porches, the fumbling hands. At first she felt nothing at all but that would change into mounting revulsion until she would pull away, although the moment before she had been unresisting. She recalled the surprise, the chagrin. "Alma, what the hell, come here, Alma, why?"

"I just don't like to be mauled, please. No, please. I'm sorry."

But, married to Ray, she longed to be a good wife, a complete wife. She accepted her failure as a fault in herself and so did Ray. After one especially trying afternoon he had said bitterly, "There is a place in Paris that has a sign which says 'There are no impotent men, only clumsy women'!"

This so agitated Alma that she felt she should heed Ray's proposal to consult a psychiatrist, Dr. Milda Loewy, who was fashionable that year. "It will be easier to talk freely to a woman," Ray had said.

Three times a week for seven months Alma had gone faithfully. Three times a week at two o'clock on the hour she had lain on a leather couch with a paper towel under her head; this was so hideously sanitary that it depressed her. Dr. Loewy, seated behind her, would unscrew the top of her fountain pen, settle in her chair

35

and wait for Alma to start talking. Once she had waited nearly the whole hour. On her desk were three framed photographs: one of Sigmund Freud and two of her children. It never ceased to astonish Alma that the doctor had managed to participate in an activity so unprofessional as producing children.

Dr. Loewy did not often speak even when asked direct questions but the sound of her breathing was as measured as a metronome and as audible.

Lying on the couch, Alma invariably hoped that she wouldn't throw up. Reluctantly, with difficulty, she picked over her life, telling repetitiously about her good-natured, hard-working father and her sweet-tempered, overworked mother, her sister Roselle, who was three years older and was married and still lived in Kensington and had two little boys and hoped for a girl. There was nothing remarkable or significant to Alma in what she laboriously remembered; it seemed to her to have been a good, cookie-jar kind of childhood. Alma talked on and on during the hour, her memory leading her to long-forgotten, apparently trivial incidents, her recounted dreams betraying incomprehensible symbols to Dr. Loewy who would lean forward, saying very little, yet forcing Alma to unwind still another skein of thought that led to . . . Alma wondered what. It was a mysterious process to her.

As the meetings proceeded, she found herself increasingly bewildered by the doctor's dark hints. She found herself in a realm of what was to her unimaginable nonsense. The dim and remote anecdotes of her childhood were being put down as evidence of an incestuous love for her father, an unconscious wish to murder her

36

mother and a consequent feeling of guilt, which had prevented her normal sexual development. So Dr. Loewy thought she wanted to sleep with her father. Poor old Pop! And as for murdering her mother, her angel of a mother whom she adored. . . . She giggled at the absurdity; then she felt sick.

Then, instead of the self-understanding that she sought, Alma just came to despise Dr. Loewy, who now reminded her of a toad. The short, stolid body in the too-tight gabardine suit, the bulging forehead, the inquisitive liquid eyes that would dilate as she regarded Alma. . . . Alma thought of her as squatting in a stagnant, scummy pool, rank with weeds, a dank place, created out of all that she heard that was evil and obscene and ugly. Alma heard herself frankly revealing this to Dr. Loewy one afternoon and then asking, "And is a toad a sexual symbol too, Dr. Loewy?"

"It is so regarded," the doctor replied calmly.

In spite of her dislike of the psychoanalyst, Alma never missed an appointment. The visits would have continued indefinitely, she supposed, if Ray hadn't left her.

Ray had left her literally, one night. It had been a Tuesday, and he simply did not come home for dinner. He had driven to Santa Barbara with a girl he had never seen until she walked into his office that afternoon and looked at him in a wanting way, a most intensely wanting way.

He tried to explain to Alma when he returned, "If sex is successfully present in a marriage, the good, lusty longing that happens between a man and a woman, then it is five percent of the marriage; if it is not present, then it becomes ninety-five percent."

Ray was gentle and generous and sorry; their parting was as amicable and unimpassioned as had been their two years of marriage.

Alma wanted to leave the house in Pacific Palisades, but she decided that she might as well stay in Hollywood since she no longer knew anyone well in New York and Kensington was, of course, forever behind her. She wanted a house of her own and Ray, who liked anything connected with houses, searched until he found a bungalow in Beverly Hills that engaged all his taste and imagination to transform it into a setting for Alma. He presented it to her along with an adequate monthly allowance and a platinum key.

"Anyone can have a gold key," he had said. "Here you are, my dear, possibly the only woman who ever shut herself *into* the Doll's House."

One of the first things that she had done when she moved into her house, the divorce papers signed, had been to cancel all future appointments with Dr. Milda Loewy.

She had no bitterness or rancor toward Ray; she supposed that she had profited from her two years with him. He always remembered to send her white roses on her birthday and a figurine of blanc de chine at Christmas to add to the collection he had started for her.

After the first strangeness of missing a man about the house had passed, Alma began to feel freer, more confident. She had to admit that Dr. Loewy had helped her in ways that she did not fully understand. That didn't mean that Alma disliked her less, it was just that she had helped as castor oil helps, though no one is expected to like it.

Sue Calder had predicted that one day it would be all right.

"Stop worrying about it," she advised. "You'll meet someone and you'll wonder what all the fuss was about. It's a matter of chemistry."

"Not as simple as that," Alma had contradicted. "Dr. Loewy says the chemical-attraction business is nonsense. That the attraction between people has to do with the patterns set down in childhood, in their relations to their parents and *theirs* to each other, with individual neuroses and repressions that affect one's choice of the love object or anima and . . ."

"I never heard so much crap in my life," Sue declared. "I don't care what the Toad says, I know what I know, put two attractive people in the same bed and they don't need the *Basic Writings of Sigmund Freud.*"

Alma laughed. "Well, since I don't seem to be having much luck Loewy's way, I might try yours."

"There'll be a man, honey," Sue counseled, "or men. You don't have to worry, not the way you look."

"But how will I know?"

"Keep trying them on for size," Sue said, "and don't look so solemn, it's really a prospect that pleases."

"I know it sounds Victorian even to use the word, but what about my reputation?" Alma asked. "Won't everyone say I'm, well—loose?"

Sue laughed wildly. "You're about as loose as Lydia Pinkham!"

Then, several months later at the Calders at a dinner party, she had met Gordon Cram. Alma had liked him at once; as soon as he entered the room she became aware of him and she was glad when he sat beside her

and talked to her. They left the Calders early and together and, driving home with him, she found herself
hoping, instead of dreading, as she usually did on such
occasions, that he would ask to come in. . . .

But there had been no need to tell Sue Calder anything. Sue had merely looked at Alma when they next
met and said, "Too bad I'm not a betting woman, Henry
could stop making pictures and retire."

"You have the soul of a madam," Alma had scolded,
feeling the color come into her cheeks, "but you would
have won the bet!"

3

. . . Now the clay was off her face, her hair free of its
band, the makeup was on so that she looked like herself
again and she had put on a white lace peignoir; Gordon
was due any minute.

"Goodnight, Mrs. Tavis," Ivy called, "I'm going
now."

"Goodnight, Ivy. Leave the side door on the latch."

She put down the atomizer of perfume and carefully applied her lipstick with a little brush. Then,
hearing Gordon's car outside she laughed and, taking
a Kleenex, she wiped the lipstick off. . . .

CHAPTER THREE THE CALDERS
had lived in one house since their marriage. It was a long house made of board and batten, painted white with a shingled roof and they had bought it because it looked as if it were in New England.

Inside it was fresh and brightly colored but hardly anything in it was new; there was a tidy clutter of things that they had collected and many books and pictures and photographs in silver frames. The third step of the stairs squeaked and the door to the kitchen stuck in wet weather but in other ways it was not a special house. It looked as if the people who lived in it did live in it and liked it.

At six o'clock of this April evening there was a suspended, contained excitement as if the house were holding its breath.

In the dining room the table was set and waiting, the silver and the white linen and the unlighted white candles gleamed palely in the dim, empty room; in the pantry the red wine to accompany the roast was being decanted and the champagne waited in two Sheffield silver coolers filled with broken, salted ice. Stiff white paper had been folded into a fan and set beneath the solid, aromatic logs in the living room fireplace to be kindled just before the guests arrived; the flowers were arranged in bowls and vases, the petals still damp and tight waiting for the moment to open and unfold and cast their small fragrance into the room. From the kitchen the odor of the roast escaped and pervaded the entire house.

The rich smell of the beef made its way upstairs to Sue Calder who sniffed it. It made her hungry, but Henry disliked the smell of cooking food and she began to worry that it would not be gone by the time he came home from the studio. She was, by her own admission, a nervous hostess, although she enjoyed having people to dinner and until the doorbell rang and the first guest arrived she was planning, rearranging, reminding herself of the innumerable details that she was capable of forgetting. "Are the red flowers on the piano?" her thoughts went, "Will the cheese be ripe enough for Henry?"

She sat now on the white-carpeted floor of her bedroom considering the twelve monogrammed place cards set out before her. Studying them as if she were telling her fortune, she picked them up and shuffled them.

"Might as well pull them out of a hat," she said to herself. "At least nobody was once married to somebody else—that makes it easier than usual."

She began to lay out the cards again. "Gordon next to Alma, no better not, Gordon next to me, George Altman on my right and then Alma and who for Alma's other side?"

Through her concentration she heard the sound of a car in the driveway and her husband's voice calling "Good evening" into the kitchen from outside. She took a lipstick from the pocket of her dressing gown and drew it blindly across her mouth. She got up from the floor, scattering the cards, and ran out of the room and down the stairs to open the door.

But she heard the crunch of the key in the lock just as she put her hand on the doorknob.

"I won," he said, "three nights in a row."

"You're getting too fast for me," she said, a little out of breath.

"No, it's you, you're getting old and infirm," he said. He put his arms around her. "What did you do to your hair now?"

"Nothing, I mean I haven't combed it out yet." She clung to him. "I'm so glad you're home."

"Let me go," he said, "have you no shame?"

"You know the answer to that," she said.

"Do you know you are having a party tonight?"

"Lord yes, did you remember to remind Gordon?"

"I did. Let's have a drink," he said, taking off his overcoat.

"Scotch and soda?"

He nodded. "Why is it so quiet?"

"The children are out. They've gone to supper with the Altman kids to save wear and tear on the kitchen."

"That means the Altmans are coming here."

"Ah, my clever one!" she said.

Henry hung up his overcoat and followed her into the

library where bottles and glasses and a thermos jug of ice were set out on a tray.

"I forgot the lemon peel," Sue said, handing him a glass.

"Doesn't matter," he sipped his drink. "Do I get Isabel Altman?"

"No, darling, you get Alma; I decided not to seat Alma and Gordon together."

"I meant to ask you how that's coming along."

"She's been seeing him every night."

"Alma really picks 'em." Henry said, "first Ray Tavis and now Gordon."

"They met in our house and I feel responsible," Sue said seriously.

"We didn't tuck them in together," Henry said, "or did you?"

The clock in the hall struck seven.

"It isn't seven," Sue cried, "no."

"You can count on the Altmans being late."

"I can't, I told them to come a half-hour earlier than the others so that they'd be only half an hour late," Sue explained.

"I understand what you are trying to tell me, but few men would."

Sue went toward the stairs. "One thing, sweetie, do try to keep George from talking about R.A.M. pictures all evening."

"George's interests are widening," Henry said. "Now he talks about television."

Sue avoided walking on the third step and stopped halfway up the staircase. "What shall I wear," she called to Henry, "the old black, the gray, or the new black?"

He pondered for a second. "The gray," he said, "and you'd better hurry, they'll be here soon. Gordon is never late."

2

"WE'RE going to be late," Gordon said, tying his dark-blue tie.

Alma shook her head, her mouth full of hair pins. "Five minutes to fix my hair," she said, "then my dress, and away we go."

"Knowing your five minutes," he said, rising, "I'll make a drink. One for you?"

"No, darling. My goodness, you get dressed fast."

"Experience," he said.

He went into the living room and opened the old rosewood cabinet that Alma had turned into a bar. He decided to have an old-fashioned and, being serious and careful about making drinks, he made them well. He selected a squat crystal glass, shook some sugar in it, splashed a few drops of bitters over that, then a little soda water and mashed the sugar with a wooden pestle, then added two ounces of Scotch exactly and a large cube of ice. He sliced an orange, squeezed a bit of the juice into the glass and finished it with a long twist of lemon peel.

Then, first stirring, then sampling the result, he regarded it with satisfaction. It also occurred to him that he felt very well indeed, alive and strong and restored. In his complete good humor with the world it was hard to recall his depressed, heavy mood of the afternoon.

He could hear Alma humming as she fixed her hair, a nameless tune of her own. It was the only sound in the small, quiet house. How pleasant it was to be alone with her! He wished that they could stay here and make dinner for themselves out of cans and whatever was in the icebox and not go to the Calders at all. He added more Scotch to his drink and went to the fireplace. He had stood in this spot the first time that he had been in the house, three months ago. He hadn't known then how significant that night was to become.

His thoughts dwelt on the first time, the discovery and the belonging, the first time and last night and an hour ago and all the times between. . . .

No other woman had made him feel just this way. Even if that was a bromide, he couldn't deny it. He had known many women and his memory was acute but there had never been quite the same shared, transmitted excitement. With all the others there had been, of course, at the time, the novelty and the urgency, but with Alma it was special. She was so lovely, loveliness clear through, he thought, to the marrow. And because he had come along at the critical moment she had said that he had changed her, helped prove Dr. Loewy and Ray Tavis to be wrong. Perhaps it would have happened with some other guy, he reasoned, but it didn't happen to be another guy and whatever was between them had grown from a chance encounter into extraordinary passion.

But he had had no forewarning that first evening that she would become so important to him.

Important. His mind held the word, questioning

it but not doubting it. Yes, she was important and that could be dangerous, could be trouble. He didn't want trouble. He took a long swallow of his drink. Louise had always predicted that something like this would happen. She'd said that it was inevitable, which was the reason for her dreading it. He remembered that night with Louise. It had been seven years ago or was it eight . . . ?

They had just had dinner together at their apartment in New York. It was winter and he remembered that they were having coffee in front of the fire. The look of the living room had pleased him that night, pleasantly shabby with use, bright with the flowers that were one of Louise's few extravagances and the gaudy jackets of new books. Louise sat opposite him watching the fire, sipping her coffee. Gordon had a good sense of not being restless, of being quite simply glad that he was there. His novel was nearly finished and he had agreed with everyone at Dover House that it would be his best.

His mind was on the novel as he said to Louise. "I've got some stuff for you to read tonight."

She looked up from her study of the fire, "Are you going out?"

"No, Jack wanted me to go to the fights at the Garden, but I thought I'd work on that Paris chapter."

"Then she must have another date."

"Lou, please," he said.

"What's her name," she continued, "there's a new one, isn't there?"

"Does her name matter?"

"If it's serious."

47

"It never is," he said, "never will be, you know that."

She got up and walked about the room. "One day it will."

"Sit down," he said, more crossly than he had intended. He was disappointed at the way his evening at home was turning out.

He watched her pace the room, already distraught—or had this been brewing all day? Usually there were signals that he could detect but she had seemed so cheerful when he came home. . . . Now suddenly her face was distorted. He knew these scenes; he'd lose his temper and later would regret it.

"Theme and variations," he thought to himself. He repeated to Louise, "Sit down, dear."

She sat down.

"I hate it when you call me dear," she said.

He didn't answer.

She spoke again, trying to control her voice. "You see I know you, Gordon. I know that some day there's going to be one you'll fall in love with."

"You're wrong."

Louise said nothing.

"What do you want me to do," he asked, "give her up?"

"What difference would that make—you'd only start another."

He poured more coffee, stirred it, tasted it. It was tepid and bitter.

"It's always been like that," Louise said. "You have an appetite for the illicit; anything clandestine tempts you, teases you. You do it as much for that as anything, I think. Because of what happened with us you think

48

you have an excuse, but that's just rationalizing it, you've always been this way, always from the beginning."

"Loulie," he said gently.

She winced at the old pet name as if she'd been struck. He hadn't called her that for a long time.

"The girl means nothing to me," he said.

"I want to know her name."

"Laura, Laura Davis."

"Is she good in bed?"

"Yes," he said, "but that doesn't mean I'm going to leave you. So let's not talk about it any more, please."

"But you'd stop it if I asked you to?"

"Yes. No one is important to me but you."

"Who writes your dialogue," she snapped, "Ernest Dowson?" She began to cry sitting up straight in the chair.

Gordon went into the kitchen and made fresh coffee, strong and hot. He brought her a cup.

"Why don't you leave me and get it over with?" she demanded. Her face was swollen and pink from her tears.

"I've told you I'll never leave you," he said. "Something happened to us that changed what we had, maybe it's ruined, maybe not. We've got to work it out in our own way."

"Your way, you mean." Louise blew her nose with a moist, ineffectual handkerchief.

Louise had huddled in her chair, looking miserable, wanting and not being wanted. All he needed to do, he knew, was to go to the chair, take her in his lap and she would be at peace. Then if he could just go upstairs with her, put her into bed and . . . but he couldn't

49

. . . The last time he had tried his failure had just made everything worse between them.

If only she had a lover, he thought. *She's still pretty.* He observed the narrow ankles, the pared waist, the shape of her breasts beneath her blouse. It had been good once and now it wasn't even possible. Not even if he were drunk, for he had discovered that he could never be drunk enough to forget.

She straightened up in the chair and looked at him. All he had to do was lean across the little space between the chairs and touch her. He didn't move nor did she.

After a while she went upstairs to bed but he went to his desk and wrote the opening and most of the notes for the story that he called "Others" when it was later published. It was the most popular story he had ever written. It first appeared in a magazine but was afterwards reprinted in anthologies and short-story collections. It became one of the inevitable titles along with "The Snows of Kilimanjaro" and "A Rose for Emily." Many people who had read nothing else of his spoke to him and wrote him letters about "Others." Only Louise never mentioned it and Gordon grew to dislike that story very much.

"Damn it," he now said half aloud. "Louise may be right. These things can get so out of hand that you lose your sense of proportion, of responsibility. It's happened to other men but I mustn't let it happen to me."

Alma called, "Will you do my dress now, darling?"

"I'm coming." He turned off the lights and went to her room.

When Gordon and Alma came out of her house a thick, pale fog had settled.

"I can't even see the car," Gordon complained.

"Don't you think fog is rather cosy?"

"Not to drive in, we'll have to crawl."

"It doesn't matter," she said. "Everyone will be late."

"We're late right now." Gordon looked at his watch. "Hooks and eyes, God save us." He grinned at her, "You all right?"

"Oh, my angel."

"Here we go," he said, starting the motor. "Out of the somewhere into the nowhere."

Gordon drove slowly, not talking. He concentrated on the traffic. Alma sat close to him on the clammy leather seat, watching him, watching his hands on the wheel. She wished that the ride would take longer than twenty minutes; enclosed in the small private darkness of the car they seemed separated from the world, safe in a temporary world where Gordon belonged to her. His shoulder brushed hers as the car turned a corner. The light from a street lamp illuminated him and she looked at the shape of his mouth. She closed her eyes and she could feel his mouth on hers, searching and restless, his teeth against her lip. She shivered, a tiny shiver of delight.

Feeling her tremble, Gordon said, "Don't be nervous."

His words surprised her. "I'm never nervous in cars," she said.

No one knows about anyone, Alma thought, *however close you are you don't know, you can't ever know, how much you long to and try to understand, however much you care, it doesn't matter, you never know about anyone else. I don't know what Gordon's thinking now, perhaps about his wife; maybe his wife gets nervous driv-*

51

ing. Oh, don't let him be thinking of her, not when he's with me.

Gordon stopped for a red light. "Fog's lifting a bit." He took his hand from the wheel and put it on her lap. "You're mighty pretty, Mrs. Tavis," he said, "in case I haven't mentioned it."

"You haven't." She held fast to his hand. "Gordon?"

"Yep?"

"Were you thinking about me just a minute ago?"

"That's right," he said. "You and the traffic problems of Wilshire Boulevard are uppermost in my mind."

"I feel good," she said, squeezing his arm. "Don't you?"

"I'll feel better when we get there."

I know so little about him, Alma thought to herself, *I want to know everything about him, what he did when he was little, what goes on in his head, his darling pre-occupied head, his hard head. I love him and I can't say it out loud. Dear God, how did I ever get into such a fix? Don't let me think of when he will go away and don't let him think about it.*

She watched his cheeks hollow as he drew on his cigarette; then he rolled the window down and tossed the cigarette out. The ember spun in the night for an instant and vanished as the car drove on.

"Only forty minutes late," Gordon remarked as they turned in at the Calders' driveway. "By Hollywood time we're still early."

Getting out of the car, he came over to the other side and opened the door.

"I don't want to go in," she said, "I want to stay with you."

52

"You'll be with me." He held out his hand.

"Let's go back home."

Gordon leaned into the car and put his arms around her as if to carry her. "You smell so good," he said.

She rested against him, not moving, not wanting him to move. The air was cold and damp with fog. It was very quiet. She put up her arm to touch his face and he felt the soft rise of her breast against his coat.

"I'm crazy about you," he said.

Her eyes gleamed in the dark, like an animal's, he thought, a beautiful, aware animal.

He put his lips on hers, not kissing her, tasting the lipstick and remembering the taste without lipstick only a little while ago, how her face had looked, wonderful and wondering.

She repaired her lipstick with a tiny golden brush.

He rubbed at his chin with a handkerchief. "Any evidence?"

"You're beautiful," she said.

They walked to the door and he rang the bell. The heavy door opened inward, the light rushed out, surged over the steps and made a path for them as they went into the house. The door closed, the light retreated and the dark returned.

CHAPTER FOUR

*H*OW *is it going?* Sue Calder asked herself halfway through dinner. Everyone was talking; the anxious bubble of heavy silence which lack of conversation causes was happily absent.

Bobby Duncan's little wife was proving a bit of a problem. *Not exactly a chatterbox,* Sue thought. She leaned forward and drew her into a conversation with Gordon. Gordon, Sue observed gratefully, was being nice to her. *She must be nervous,* Sue thought, *but why does she wear her hair like that? We must do something about it. Cut it, or something. I never did like hair that color. Graham cracker.*

Now that Peggy Duncan was launched with Gordon, Sue turned her attention to others. Everyone was eating. She looked down the length of the table (how pretty the table is) through the white candles, over the long bowl of flowers, to see if Henry were pleased or not pleased.

He was twirling the wineglass by its stem, listening to Jean Fielding. Jean was leaning toward him, baring her beautiful bosom and her beautiful teeth, talking in her energetic yet intensely intimate way. *The practically-in-your-lap manner,* Sue thought, remembering that she had once made Jean angry by describing her attitude toward men as a cross between a tart and the captain of a girls' hockey team.

Sue slid a little in her chair, searching with her foot for the buzzer. It was embedded in the carpet in a spot she had selected but whenever she needed it she could never find it. *The roast should be passed again,* she thought. Then she found the buzzer and pressed triumphantly, vehemently.

"Take some of the rare," she said to Gordon, "that's too done for you."

"No, it's perfect. I always eat too much here," he said. "To my mind," Gordon raised his glass, "you set the finest table in the county, Mrs. Calder, ma'am."

"Can you see if Henry has eaten anything?" she whispered.

Gordon tilted his chair backwards. "Clean plate," he reported, "relax. Is he still a fussy eater?"

"He loves food but he hates home-cooking."

"That's what happens to women who marry bachelors," Gordon said. "They never can forget the infinite variety of the restaurant menu, which age cannot wither nor custom stale."

"I think I'm breaking his spirit, though. He hasn't made crêpes Suzette at the table in a year, not since the night he upset the chafing dish and nearly set the house on fire. Weren't you here that night?"

"I was spared," Gordon said, "and so was Henry. I would have had him put under arrest as an incendiary."

55

"Next time marry a fellow who doesn't know the difference between potato soup and vichysoisse," George Altman joined in. "Don't marry a gourmet."

"It's too late," Sue said, smiling.

"How long have you been married now?" George asked. "I can't remember you two not together."

"Ten years and a little."

"That's a long time for Hollywood."

"Or any place."

"Amen."

"Sue, if you know why the Westleys are separating," Isabel Altman called from the other end of the table, "don't hold out."

"I don't know anything about it. They're always slipping in and out of wedlock."

"Don't worry, dear, she just wants to wait till the women get together," George Altman observed to his wife.

"The curious thing is," Sue mused to Gordon, "it's not the reasons that people separate I'm interested in; it's what keeps them together."

Gordon found himself on guard. Was she trying to find out about his marriage or was this dinner-table talk? He was about to reply when she said, "We'll get salad if I ever find that buzzer again. Is it near your foot, Gordon?"

Alma helped herself to salad from the big wooden bowl, hearing but not listening to what George Altman was saying. She had known George since she had first come to Hollywood. He was the "A" of R.A.M. Studios where Ray Tavis had been working at the time of their marriage and George and his wife, Isabel, had been

56

kind to Alma during and after her life with Ray. She was fond of them but tonight she was too involved in her own emotions to do more than make vague answers whenever his voice stopped questioningly.

She looked over at Gordon, who was spreading cheese on a toasted biscuit.

"To look at a man and feel as I do this minute," she thought, "whatever happens, it's worth it."

George's voice stopped and she made an answer, "You're right, Tony certainly was miscast."

The red-wine glasses and the salad plates were being removed when Sue noticed that Jean Fielding had turned from Henry. She and Bob Duncan were talking to each other as if they were the only people in the room and it was not a dining room. On Peggy Duncan's face there was a faintly stricken expression.

"So he's started already," Sue thought.

George Altman was asking Sue something and she listened as the dessert plates were set down. They were her favorites of fluted, flowered china. *The dessert*, she prayed privately, *please make Henry not hate the dessert*.

Aloud she answered George, "No, I don't agree at all with you and Alma, I think Tony was wonderful for the part."

"This dessert," Isabel Altman cried, "is the best thing I've ever tasted!"

Silently she wondered if Sue could be coaxed into giving her the recipe. *If I let her have my ox-tail soup maybe she'll trade*, she figured to herself.

Jean Fielding refused the dessert reluctantly. "I crave it," she said, "but I'm wearing one of those tighter-than-skin numbers tomorrow, all black sequins, so not for me."

She was, Jean thought, as she watched the others eat, tired of worrying about her figure, tired of massages and facials; she was a good actress, still a favorite with the exhibitors and even with the critics, but she had to take care of her weight or she'd soon find herself playing character parts.

While Bobby Duncan was spreading chocolate sauce over his plate, Jean opened her purse and looked into the mirror fastened to the lid. With the cold eye of a housewife estimating a melon she looked at her face. Her lipstick was smudged a bit in the left corner. She removed it with a barely perceptible motion and her mouth was again pristine and glossy. She had capitalized on that full mouth, exaggerated it as she had the wide-apart eyes, the bold, unplucked eyebrows. She had set a style for looks that had been copied all over the country. Many of the facsimiles had come to Hollywood and gone away again but she remained and she intended to remain in just the spot that she had made for herself for as long as she could.

She closed her bag and watched Bobby Duncan chewing. He was a pretty boy and young enough not to have to worry about his weight. Too young? She considered the question.

Henry Calder looked down the length of the table; he held his untouched champagne glass in his hand, trying to catch Sue's eye. *Dinner was superb*, Henry thought, *but Sue doesn't care whether I like it or not, she isn't even looking to see if I like the dessert.*

Bob doesn't love me any more, Peggy Duncan told herself, feeling such misery that she couldn't enjoy the lovely dessert or talk to the pleasant man beside her who wrote books or do anything but stare at her husband and Jean Fielding. *He's tired of me already. Oh, I wish I was home, away from these people. I wish I was dead, then he'd be sorry. Oh, Bobby, Bobby, why don't you laugh that way with me?*

Gordon waited until Sue was occupied with George and then he allowed himself to look at Alma. *I know all about her, not only do I know that she is wearing nothing at all under that dress, but I know how to fasten the dress, all those little hooks and eyes that took so long.*

Alma felt him looking at her, though she was not looking at him. The color came into her face and she forgot what she had been talking about.

I want to kiss her, he thought, *among other things.* He thought of the moment in his car, outside the house. Then he realized that nobody was talking to Peggy Duncan.

"Do you like it out here or do you miss New York?" he asked.

"Oh, I love it here," she said, "don't you?"

"I'm a Sixtieth Street man and I miss the city."

"You do?" She looked surprised. "You're the first person I've met in California who does, Mr. Cram."

"I like to see people walking," he said. "If they catch you on foot out here they arrest you."

She laughed at him and stopped looking at her husband and Jean Fielding.

"Where did you live in New York?" Gordon asked.

59

"In Great Neck with the family but it isn't far, you know, and I used to come into town all the time and . . ."

Nice little kid, Gordon thought, *too bad she didn't stay in Great Neck.*

Sue observed that everyone but Jean took a second helping of the dessert. And everyone was talking. She was sorry that the Rodgers, those unflagging talkers, had made a mistake about the date and couldn't come in till after dinner, but they didn't seem to be needed. She sipped her champagne, pleased about her party. Her two main worries, food and conversation, were fading and she could now allow the nervous hostess to recede and begin to enjoy herself. Then she realized that Henry was looking at her and that she was looking at him— and that it was nice.

Jean turned from looking into Bob Duncan's bright blue eyes to Henry to find him beaming at his wife. *I wonder if he's still in love with her after all this time.* Sue was smart about men, Jean had always told her so, and Sue had laughed and said, "Just the same, I'm glad you checked Henry off the list before my time."

"Sue and I understand each other," Jean said to Henry.

"Why not? You're both fine girls," he said, smiling.

"Do you really mean that?"

Bobby Duncan touched her arm lightly above the elbow. "Talk to me," he commanded.

Too young, definitely too young, Jean was thinking

60

as she smiled at him, her special, slow smile. He caught his breath. *But rather sweet*, she thought.

"It's terrible," he was saying, "you and I only meet in people's houses. I never have a chance."

"Don't you, Bobby?"

"No," he said. "When we first met, on the lot—you probably don't remember," he waited.

She didn't remember, but she said, "Of course I remember. What about it?"

"Well," he continued, in a low, private voice, "well, you were married then, Jeanie, and I'm married now."

"What bad timing," she said, and this time she didn't smile.

The same routine, she thought, letting his hand brush her fingers. She looked at Rip Dudley, who had brought her, but had to leave immediately after dinner. Not that it mattered, Rip was an old friend and that was all but it was dull of Sue Calder not to have got someone for tonight that she could have some fun with, someone more interesting than old Rip. Rip was sexually neutral, not even a candidly contented homo. What a bore the neutrals were—or should one feel sorry for them? Now Gordon Cram, that was something else again. She patted the soft curls at the back of her head. There was something about him, the shoulders, she thought, and the way he looked right at you when he talked, something vital and alive that made you think it might be fun, might be considerably more than fun. She could hear him laughing now at Bobby's wife and the sound of his laughter, very male laughter, stirred something in her that was half-asleep. After dinner, she promised herself, she'd talk with him. Why hadn't Sue asked him to call for her, instead of Rip? That would have made it so simple, because then he would have taken her home. But perhaps Sue wanted him for her friend Alma—as if Gordon Cram could want Alma Tavis! She was pretty enough, but everyone knew why Ray Tavis had left her. She was a cold potato. Rip and Alma would make the perfect pair. Two cold potatoes.

"What are you thinking about, Jeanie?" Bobby whispered, his hand on her knee.

"About potatoes," she said.

Gordon listened to Peggy Duncan talk about Smith College, where her mother and aunt and cousin had gone and where she would have been tonight if she hadn't married Bob.

"Smith's a good place," Gordon said, "I once knew a girl who went to Smith but that was years ago."

"What was her name? Maybe Mother knew her."

"That makes a man feel like a lad," Gordon thought. "Her name was Helen," he said, "that was a very popular name among the Neanderthal women."

"Helen Neanderthal—?"

"That was it," Gordon smiled at her. "You're a sweet child and I shall be your Uncle Gordon."

What *was* her name? Helen, Helen . . . he'd written her a letter twice a week from an autumn to the spring following when she'd become engaged to a boy at Princeton and he'd felt terrible about it. Now he couldn't remember her name or anything about her except that she had red hair and beautiful legs and wouldn't go to bed with him although they had spent a great deal of time talking it over in the back seat of parked cars.

Helen Adams, no, but it did begin with an A, Abbott, Adler, Abernathy, Allen, Ames, Arbuthnot . . . Neander-thal.

How extraordinarily little one remembered, even people with those capacious, infallible freak memories, even they must forget so much, miles of unremembered hours, jokes, tears, frights, boredoms and all the days of just getting up and living the day through and going to bed again, those were forgotten. It was simple enough to remember anguish or great delight but even those faded with time, which was probably merciful; the weight would be otherwise unsupportable.

His eyes rested on Alma. *Will I forget you? Will I become an old man, sour, juiceless, smoking denico-tinized cigarettes, living my life out in a clement and inexpensive resort? Will I not remember all things I felt acutely, the war, or the awful time of being a child, or the time I went to Nassau with Louise, the first time either of us had been anywhere together, or the day that Will Tucker at Dover House accepted the first book and gave me an advance, or the time I didn't sell that story to Collier's, or that I once talked about studying Greek with Louise (we were going to take a course together at night), or my father and how little I forgive him and all the books I've read and the books I've written and all the girls and you, Alma Tavis, will I one day be so old and cold and withered that I will forget you . . . ?*

Gordon put down his spoon and looked at her with a forlorn apprehension. Then he forgot about the old man he might become and his thoughts went to the very first time he had ever seen Alma three months ago. It seemed farther away than that and yet so immediate that

63

he saw it all sharply in focus, as if he were watching a scene on a stage. . . .

She had been sitting on a sofa near the fire in the Calders' living room, talking to Henry. She sat as he later learned she always sat, as if she were being photographed for a fashion magazine. He remembered the gray velvet she had worn, though he usually didn't pay much attention to women's clothes. He liked to see girls wearing pretty dresses that gave some clue to how they would look not wearing anything, yet he thought that he could draw every detail of that dress, the soft material had been cut away from her shoulders to reveal the curve of her breasts and the wide skirt was draped around her on the sofa. Her skin against the dove-gray velvet had the paleness of a pearl. Gordon had wondered if she were really blonde; he had seen that pallor with black hair but never with hair of dark gold. It was brushed back severely, pinned at the top of her head. He thought that provocative. It set him to picturing it unpinned, free and wanton, on a pillow, perhaps.

Ray Tavis was a dope to give that up, he thought.

She was quiet, he noticed, almost shy but without the coy implications of shyness. She was completely composed and, Gordon decided, rather remote. As far as he was concerned, this withdrawn manner detracted from Mrs. Tavis. *Serenity is all very well for a woman in a novel,* Gordon said to himself, *but in life it bores me.*

There was a cast of sadness over her, like a thin rainless shadow over the bright enamel of a summer day. *Maybe she's unhappy about that bastard Tavis,* Gordon thought. Then he had gone to find Sue Calder.

She was in the library mixing martinis in a pitcher.

64

"Too dark, put in more gin," he said, "and tell me about her." There was no need to be more explicit with Sue. She would know whom and what he meant.

"It's too bad she's so homely," Sue said, "she has a heart of gold."

"Come on, tell me."

"What do you want to know?"

As it wasn't like Sue to be evasive, Gordon became more interested.

"Legs?" he asked. "You can't see in long dresses."

"Are legs important with that face?"

"They are important with any face. Now then, good or not so good, or awful?"

"Superb," Sue said.

"The hair, is it true?"

"That color can't be duplicated with dye," Sue said. "It's a natural blessing, like dimples."

"An Edwardian color."

"Exactly." She looked pleased with him. "Like Irene Forsyte, remember?"

"Dead leaves, wasn't that it?"

"Yes, *feuilles mortes.*"

"Sounds better in French."

"What doesn't?" asked Sue.

He laughed at her, feeling fond of her, of her house and the Scotch old-fashioned he was drinking and of the good dinner he was going to eat. It was one of those moments of well-being, of a sense of the richness and joy possible in life.

"You join the fray," Sue said, "and let me fix your drink."

"I'll wait," he said. "I like to talk to you. How could Ray Tavis have walked out on that, or did he?"

Sue shrugged.

"I never liked him," Gordon said. "I don't know him well, but in my opinion he's over-rated as a director and pompous as a person."

"It's simple. I don't like Ray because he doesn't like me," Sue said, "but Alma's quite a girl."

"Worst of all," said Gordon, taking the drink from Sue, "he rewrites the dialogue on the set. The unholy sin."

"Save your wrath for the Screen Writers' Guild."

"To finish my thought," Gordon went on, "now that I've seen the former Mrs. Tavis, I think he must be out of his mind."

At dinner he had studied Alma, trying to decipher the riddle he sensed was there. After a while he concluded that the appropriate slogan was "untouched by human hands."

Later in the evening he had said to her, "You probably know that we're among parlor-game fiends, so shall we hide in the library?"

He discovered that she was easy to talk to, that she became more animated when one was alone with her. The cool cloak of her manner changed, slightly, subtly and he began to suspect that the remoteness was an attitude, a possible remnant of Ray Tavis's coaching.

Perhaps no one had asked her for more than to sit still and be admired. *I'd ask for more*, thought Gordon, *a lot more*. He felt that there was kindness in her and generosity and spirit, but something about her was

66

lacking. . . . He searched for the word, looking in the green-gray eyes. . . .

He had said, "Let's get out of here."

She had looked at him. "Alright," she said.

"I'll go out through the garden," he said, "you get your coat and meet me in front of the house."

She nodded, a faint color coming into her cheeks.

He had a sudden feeling of excitement. He knew what he intended to do and he surmised that she did too but it seemed to promise more than the inevitable. There was something special about her and he was going to find out what it was. . . .

And he had found out, he now thought, eating the last rich spoonful of the Calders' dessert. Here, now, about three months later, he found himself in this peculiar state of mind. He meditated on his restlessness at the studio during the melancholy afternoon. His life was emotionally untidy, *That sounds like Louise,* he thought, *that's one of her phrases, emotionally untidy.*

"I'm going to leave you now to cigars and dubious anecdotes," Sue said, rising. "Jeanie, Alma, Isabel, Peggy, come along. Good-bye, gentlemen."

She paused beside Henry's chair.

"Good-bye, cutie," he said and patted her bottom.

CHAPTER FIVE "WHAT a lovely room,
Mrs. Calder!" Peggy Duncan exclaimed as they filed into
the bedroom. "This house doesn't look a bit like a Hollywood house. I hope you don't mind my saying so."

"I love your saying so," Sue said, smiling at her. She
opened the door that led into the bathroom, "Right in
here, if you're interested."

"She's a dear little person," Isabel Altman murmured
as the door closed behind Peggy.

"God help her," Sue said, "married to him."

"Do you still dislike actors' wives after all these
years?"

"I'm opposed to wives," Sue declared, "actors' wives
especially, the way they watch their men—not that they
don't have cause in this town." Sue made a point of
not looking at Jean. "But they should keep the pretty
boys at home or use muzzles and leads when they take
them out."

68

"Well, Susie, you can like me now," Jean announced. "I am no longer a wife."

"Is your divorce final?"

"As of yesterday at noon."

"You'll be married again next month," Isabel and Alma cried in unison.

"Nope, three times and marriage is out," Jean denied emphatically. "It is not for me."

"You have your profession," Alma said, a trifle wistfully.

"Please," said Jean, "let's call it a career."

"Career or profession or gainful employment or just plain job isn't enough, we all need a man," Sue stated.

"I'm not giving up men, dear, just matrimony."

"Weren't you once married to an actor?" Isabel asked Jean.

"To my everlasting shame. I was too young to know better."

"I remember now, of course," Isabel said. "Stanley Farrell. My Lord, he was good-looking."

"Wasn't he?" Jean said, "and the low-life of the world. We were married three years and all I ever got from him was a taste for Turkish cigarettes. I still smoke them." She opened her square jewelled box, took out an oval, cork-tipped cigarette and looked at it. "Among my souvenirs."

"What happened to him?" Alma asked.

"Somebody shot him," Jean said, "which was what he deserved. He got out of town and I haven't heard a word from him since. We had a very unstylish, unfriendly divorce."

Isabel, having emptied her purse of assorted gold

69

boxes and trinkets, said, "I have everything I own in this bag but a lipstick. Do you happen to have a dark one, Sue?"

Peggy Duncan came out of the bathroom. "Sorry to be so long," she apologized, "I was admiring the pink glass. Is it Bristol?"

"Am I next or is anyone else desperate?" Jean asked.

"Go ahead, Jeanie," said Sue, "yes, it is Bristol."

"Mother collects the blue," Peggy said.

"Jean's looking well, I think," Isabel said, "but those circles! What *can* she be doing?"

"I think she's gorgeous," Peggy put in, "I'm so thrilled to meet her, it's the funniest thing my meeting her, why when I was a little girl . . ."

"She was my favorite actress," Sue finished the sentence for her. "But I wouldn't tell her."

"Bless her wee heart," Isabel whispered to Alma, "is she dumb or what?"

"Just young. She'll get over that," Alma said.

There was something touching about the girl; the way she looked at Bobby when he was behaving so obviously with Jean. What would Hollywood do to her—toughen her up or send her running home to mother in Great Neck?—Alma wondered to herself.

"I wouldn't blame any man for being attracted to her," Peggy was saying, looking miserable, "she's so glamorous, I mean."

Alma was relieved to hear Sue changing the subject. "Bobby tells me you're doing wonders with the house."

"Oh, I hope you'll come and see it, Mrs. Calder."

Alma leaned back on Sue's big white bed.

Isabel looked at her and said, "You look divine. Who else in the world could wear that color, lilac, isn't it?"

"Pale violet they called it at Carnegie's." Alma lifted a petal of the pleated skirt toward the lamp.

"I'd call it mauve," Sue said.

"Orchid?" Peggy suggested.

"No, that's for bathroom tiles."

"Whatever color it is, I'd look like hell in it," Isabel said. "Did you find a lipstick, Sue?"

"Use mine, it's rather dark," Jean offered as she came back into the room. "Is it cold in here or is it me?" She continued, stroking her arms.

Sue went to the fire and put on another log. "Henry can't sleep unless the temperature is sub-zero."

"You know what they say about cold climates," Jean said.

"Is that true? Then why are there so few Eskimos?"

Jean laughed and looked at herself in the mirror over the mantel, "I can't wait till I finish the picture and let my hair grow out. I loathe this color, but they like it for technicolor."

Her hair was an odd color, Sue thought, the same soft pink-brown of a spoiled red banana.

"Whatever became of red bananas?" she said aloud. "You never see them anymore."

"New pictures of the children?" Jean asked, picking up a folder of photographs.

"A new boy at the studio took them."

Jean and Peggy looked at the pictures with the unfeigned admiration of anyone who doesn't have a child.

"You'll be having a baby soon, I suppose," Jean said

to Peggy, aware of her for perhaps the first time that evening.

"Oh, I don't know," Peggy replied, her face rosy at Jean's attention. "We haven't been married long and Mother says . . ."

"Forget what Mother says," Isabel Altman joined their conversation. "Mother is in Great Neck, you're here."

"Do you believe in having children right away, Mrs. Altman?"

"Soon as it's decent, Peggy, nothing like it to hold a man."

"Rot," Sue contradicted, "if a marriage needs children to hold it then it's not much of a marriage."

"Sue's right," Jean spoke impatiently, "she knows what holds men." Jean studied Peggy as if she were going to hypnotize her. "And if you don't know, then you'd better learn. Let children wait for a while."

"Bobby wants six, he says."

"They all *say* that," Jean said, "keep stalling, take my advice."

"By all means take Jean's advice," Isabel rose, nettled. "I've only been married to the same man for a mere fifteen years."

"Going to try for twenty?" Jean inquired.

Before Isabel could answer, Peggy said, "I guess you never had the time to have a baby, Miss Fielding."

"I had the time, just never had the husband long enough."

They all laughed, including Isabel, and the tension evaporated. *God help women,* Sue thought. *They need it.*

"But I wouldn't care about children or anything,"

Peggy said, emboldened by Jean's interest, "if I had the thrilling life you have."

"Thrilling life," Jean laughed shortly. "I slave like a dog for two hundred and seventy-five thousand dollars a year; and after taxes I can keep nineteen if my business manager is smart enough. And I've got more out-of-work relatives than anybody in the U.S.A."

"No more than George Altman," Isabel said with feeling.

"George has the studio to take up the slack. He can hire his relatives. His dopey nephew, Johnny, is assistant casting director. His sister's husband—the one who drinks—handles censorship troubles with the Breen office. They're all over the place and don't cost *him* a cent. The stockholders pay. But I've really got to help out—another way of saying support. Why, I've even got custody of my ex-in-laws."

"You have no idea how many Altmans there are," Isabel still insisted sadly, "one cousin in Chicago just had triplets."

"Spiteful of her," Sue said.

"I'd like to buy a pair of stockings just once and have someone else pay for them," Jean said. "I never get anything from anybody but thanks."

"And I always thought that actresses got wonderful loot," Sue said.

Jean raised her arm so that the diamond and sapphire bracelet slipped back from her wrist. "This trinket was a wedding present from my former husband. I was charmed till the bill came."

"You're disillusioning us, Jeanie."

"I'm disillusioned myself," she shook her head, "and

when people say 'what can we possibly give you, you have everything,' then I really burn."

"But don't you have everything? Haven't you really?" Peggy asked.

"I don't know. I haven't taken inventory lately."

"Anyhow, I think it would be so exciting, your life, I mean your job," Peggy said, her eyes bright.

"You wouldn't after a few months of it and I've had years."

"But being on the screen, being so famous, your picture all over the place, being a celebrity and the love scenes with those beautiful men."

"Well, I guess there are compensations to every job. The men are my compensation. But you have to watch them in the love scenes or all that the camera will ever see is the back of your head. Never trust an actor in a love scene if there's a camera going. To protect yourself you and the director have to be on good terms, if you follow me. They may not be as pretty as the leading men but they do take care of you in the close-ups. Of course, sometimes they get carried away, the actors I mean. They're only human after all," Jean smiled at the reflection. "Last year I was doing a picture with Fred Tower and he really got in the mood one day. Tore the front of my dress right off. And the look on his face! My God, it was a terrific scene but Breen made them cut it. I hardly knew Fred then, but after that, well . . ."

"Honestly, Jean is the limit," Isabel murmured to Sue, "talking that way to a child."

"The child is married."

"Which Jean also seemed to forget at dinner," Isabel

replied crisply. "What's the matter with her anyway—he's years younger than she is. Is she getting anxious?"

"No more than usual."

"I always forget about Henry and Jean," Isabel murmured, "or I wouldn't mention it, Sue dear."

"I know you wouldn't, Isabel dear."

"Oh, Sue," Jean said, "what's this about the Westleys separating? You know you know."

"Of course I know, but I didn't want to mention it at the table. Men are such gossips, it would be all over town tomorrow."

"Well, tell now," Isabel urged.

"It's dreadful," Sue said, "and ludicrous. I asked Rose to come tonight but she won't leave the house in case Dickie should come back or telephone."

"*He* left?"

"In a way, yes. Rose heard there was an antique shop in the Valley where they had some milk-glass plates. So one day last week, I think it was Thursday, she drove over to look at them," Sue related. "She asked me to go with her but fortunately I couldn't. Well, you know how many motels there are along Ventura Boulevard," Sue paused to light a cigarette.

"Sue, please, hurry up."

"Well, it's the most hideous coincidence. Rose was parking in front of the shop and suddenly she saw Dick driving out of a motel which was actually right next door. She recognized him immediately."

"Why wouldn't she?" Jean asked, "he's her husband."

"Well, she didn't expect to see him driving out of a motel at three o'clock in the afternoon."

"Was he alone?"

75

"No, a girl was with him."

"He certainly wouldn't be at a motel all by himself," said Alma.

"Anyhow it was awful. Rose honked her horn without thinking about it. Dick saw her but kept on going and poor silly Rose followed him! They went over Coldwater Canyon—you know how twisty and winding that is—poor Rose was car-sick and half out of her mind but she kept on. He went like crazy. It's a miracle they weren't killed."

"Did she catch up with him?"

"On the Beverly side of Coldwater, just opposite the fire station."

"How appropriate," Jean said.

"Don't stop now," Isabel cried.

"Rose got out of her car and made a terrible scene. She hit Dick in the face with her pocketbook and a fifty-cent piece fell out. The girl picked it up and handed it to Rose who spit at her and said, 'Keep it, it's your fee!'"

"No!" they all said at once.

"Poor Rose, she wants to forget the whole thing, but Dick is angry at the way she behaved. He's left the house and says he wants a divorce. They'll make up, though. The girl means nothing to Dick, and Rose is ashamed of herself. By the way, she wants to sell her milk-glass collection. She can't bear the sight of it."

"What a fool poor Rose is," Isabel remarked. "I always said it would never last and I was matron of honor at the wedding."

"Dick's the fool," Jean said. "When I used to know

him he had an apartment in Hollywood. Rose never knew a thing about it."

Isabel and Sue exchanged a look.

"Who was the girl?" Alma asked, "she must be in shock."

"A girl called Cindy Dobbs. Rose says she wants to be in pictures."

"Sounds like she'll make it," Jean said.

"My goodness," said Peggy Duncan. "My goodness!"

"Things like this happen in East Orange," Jean said.

"Great Neck," corrected Peggy, "the Oranges are in New Jersey."

"I'll bet the same thing goes on there anyway," Jean said, exhaling a cloud of smoke.

Isabel was frowning. "Cindy Dobbs," she repeated, "Cindy Dobbs. I know I've heard that name."

Jean looked at Sue meaningly; almost imperceptibly Sue shook her head.

Jean, thwarted as she was about to speak, leaned over instead and removed her left shoe. "These pumps kill my feet," she said.

"Aren't they pretty!" Alma said, "I'd like a pair in black."

"Very ladylike," Isabel commented, "I'm surprised to see you wearing them, Jean."

Sue asked quickly, "Did you like the dessert, Isabel?"

"Divine. I was going to ask, do you use unsweetened chocolate?"

"I'll send you the recipe," Sue promised. "I got it out of *Vogue* a few months ago."

Alma got up and went toward the bathroom door. "Is it my turn now, Susie?"

77

Sue nodded and followed her.

"Whew," Sue said, closing the door, "those two will skin each other alive one of these days. I hope it doesn't happen in my house."

"They're both so nice, really."

"Yes, but between them they don't have the brain of a peafowl." She brushed some powder from her skirt. "And how are things with you, my pet?"

"Heaven," Alma said, "bliss."

What a pity, Sue thought, *that of all men it had to be Gordon.* He'd leave Hollywood as soon as he finished the script and the affair would end as had all the others that Sue knew about. *Instead of behaving like a madam I should have warned her, I should have said, "Run, Alma, run, this is trouble walking in shoe leather, don't answer the phone, run, run, run." But I wanted her to learn about life and from an expert and now it's all leading up to Gordon's usual disappearing act at which he makes Houdini look butter-fingered.*

But Alma was happily unaware of Sue's thoughts. She smiled as she said, "I have something to tell you that will amuse you. Gordon asked me tonight if I'd told you about us."

Sue took off her long pearl earring and rubbed her ear lobe. "For a man who has known a lot of women he certainly doesn't know much about them."

"Wasn't all that divorce talk at dinner peculiar?" Alma asked.

"You mean peculiar that Gordon didn't join in it?"

"Were you talking to him?"

"I was saying that it wasn't what separated people

78

that interested me half as much as what kept them to-gether," Sue said.

"He probably thought that you were prying."

"I was."

"Do you think he will ever leave her?"

"It's reached that stage, has it?"

Alma nodded.

"Come to lunch tomorrow."

"I'd like that," Alma said, "but I know right now that you think he won't ever leave her."

Sue said gently, "He never has."

Alma's face changed.

"I don't think that you should be the one to break it up," Sue said quickly. "Let's find one with no strings and no connections."

"I thought that you approved?" Alma looked surprised.

Sue reached for two cigarettes and gave one to Alma.

"When I thought that it was going to be an extended one-night stand, I was pleased. I thought in my feeble-minded way that it might be good for you. I didn't expect that you'd be so damn serious about it." Sue lit her own cigarette, then Alma's, and went on, "Shut me off whenever you want, but ever since I've known Gordon he has had a girl for a while, then he finds an-other girl. He's Old Unfaithful and he has a wife safely stashed away so that nobody can play for keeps."

"That doesn't prove he's happy with her," Alma said. "They haven't really lived together for years, Gordon told me."

"Did he tell you why?"

"No," Alma said, "you know Gordon."

"I'm amazed he told you that much," Sue said.

"But just the same I could make him a good wife. I know he'd be different with me."

"Dear God, why do they always say that when they're in love with married men?" Sue groaned.

"I don't consider it a real marriage," Alma persisted.

"It's a hell of a responsibility breaking up any kind of a marriage," Sue said. "I don't want to preach, but I do believe that."

"I didn't mean it to turn out this way," Alma spoke slowly, "I thought that I could manage it."

"I'm sure you can," Sue said with a conviction she was far from feeling. "We'd better go downstairs. The Rodgers will be coming."

"One thing I must ask you before we go. Do you think he was ever really in love with her?"

"I imagine he was," Sue played with the strand of pearls at her throat.

"Have you seen them together?" Alma asked.

"Only a couple of times in New York. She never comes out here."

"What is she like?" Alma asked apprehensively.

Sue tried to remember Louise Cram. "She seemed sad, a sadness that was stamped on her face, no—stamped is external and this was something inside. I assure you it didn't make for a gay evening."

"Is she attractive?"

"You wouldn't think so," Sue said. "She looks like the kind of woman who would use pine essence in her tub."

"Oh, Sue," Alma laughed at her. Then she stopped laughing. "How was she to Gordon?"

"She softened a little with him and you could see how vulnerable she was."

"Oh," said Alma.

"It seemed as though she'd been terribly hurt some-where along the line. I don't know or I'd tell you."

"She probably helps Gordon with his work and maybe that's what keeps them together."

"Perhaps," Sue agreed, "but I've always had the feel-ing there was more to it."

"How was he to her—tell me just that and I'll let you go."

"He was kind to her," Sue said, "unnaturally kind."

She left the room first and joined the others so as not to have to see Alma's face.

Alma felt cold suddenly. She moved to the bedroom and found that the women had gone. She stood by the fire holding her hands out to the blaze. *It's going to come to nothing,* she admitted wearily, *like every-thing else in my life, it will end in emptiness and I'll be alone again.*

She looked at Sue's room. *Some women are lucky, like my sister, like Sue, a husband she's crazy about and children and a busy, happy life.*

She stared at the wide, white-curtained bed. Every night Sue could get in that bed and know that she was not alone, that she had someone to talk to and quarrel and make up with and if she awakened in the night Henry would be there the whole night through and still in the morning.

Alma covered her face, resisting tears. *Gordon will go, Sue is right.* Could she ever love anyone else, having loved only once, such a passionate love? It was un-

81

thinkable that there could be another. Sue would laugh at her and say, "Don't be quaint, of course there will be another."

Perhaps it would be wise to end it now, to leave him first, she thought, *before he leaves me and goes back to his wife.* His wife, nameless, faceless to Alma but who could claim him any time. *After all, they've been married a long time. Whatever he says to me in bed, he's said to her.*

She sat down. "Oh, my God."

After a few moments, she went back into the bathroom and splashed her face with cold water. Then she powdered it, put on some perfume and thought about going downstairs.

2

THE MEN were still in the dining room which by now was fogged by the smoke of four excellent cigars. They had all moved to new seats toward the head of the table and sat thickly grouped around Henry with something of the atmosphere of an all-night poker game. There was a balloon glass of *fine* in front of each man except Bobby Duncan who had a creme de menthe in crushed ice which he was sucking rather noisily through two red straws. The conversation was loud and dominated at the moment by George Altman.

"I tell you that television as national entertainment is a joke. For special news and sports events, stuff like that, okay. But for fun, forget it. It will be the biggest bust since the Mississippi Bubble . . ."

Gordon interrupted, "Seems to me that's what most of you experts out here said about the talkies back in '29."

"*Altogether* different!" George was not thwarted.

As Henry listened he silently recalled that George Altman had once told Harry Warner that sound pictures were a fad that wouldn't last a year.

"Television as entertainment," George was saying, "would force people to stay home all the time. Americans hate to stay home, always have, too damn dull. Movies satisfy the appetite for adventure that is the biggest part of the American character . . . All right, so it's a vicarious satisfaction but that's better than none. That's better than staying cooped up with the family."

Bobby looked shocked. "You certainly don't think much of the American home!"

There was a pause as George meditated and sniffed his brandy. The comment was being weighed by him patiently with due consideration of its source. "Don't misunderstand me, Bob," he gently went on, "I have lots of respect for the American family. But homes, wherever you find them I guess, all have some trouble and complications. In spite of all the love that's going on inside and all the loyalty and all the other things that folks turn to when they're in trouble or sick, there's always the moments when you want out. And that's when you want your fun, fun alone, fun full of some kind of promise, beyond the horizon. Call it any damn thing you want, it ain't television with all the damn kids whose nose you've been wiping all day rolling around on the best chairs, telling you what program they want. Anyway, you'll see."

I wonder, Henry thought to himself. He was about to say it aloud but stopped himself, realizing that such arguments got nowhere. The leaders of Hollywood were forever making predictions they had to eat and right now who could have any assurance about anything? At this very moment as they sat here, a national convention of theater owners were holding a meeting at the Ambassador Hotel and the only exhibits of the evening were not the best new pictures but the ten latest types of popcorn-vending machines. One was reported to remove the stink of the stale butter, an industry problem. What a business!

Gordon had hardly listened. Experts, wherever they were, bored him. The Army generals who turned down the machine gun, the admirals who testified that no bomb would ever sink a battleship, the bankers in high Wall Street places who had to jump from even higher places after October 1929, Colonel Lindbergh who predicted that England would never resist the German air force, Senator Borah who stated solemnly to the Senate in August 1939 that there "would be no war" in Europe, experts all, lords of their trades, what the hell did any of them know? He dismissed all prophets and his thoughts turned to his own future. His own immediate future. Tonight, for instance. He wished Alma and the others would come down from upstairs.

"Let's take our brandy into the library," said Henry, reading his mind, "the girls won't be much longer."

Slowly they rose and accompanied him, talking as they went.

"All those books," Bobby Duncan shook his head at

the shelves that reached from floor to ceiling, "like a public library."

"Not props either," George Altman added, tapping a row to prove his point. "Remember Tiny Redder's house, all false fronts, not a real book in the place except *Flossie, A Virgin of Sixteen* and the *Saturday Evening Post.*"

"Henry Calder, the publisher's friend," Gordon said.

"You don't read them all, do you, Henry?" asked Bobby. "You couldn't have read all these books. How could a guy like you find the time? I'm the world's slowest reader, I guess, got so much else to do."

"What?" Gordon asked.

"When I'm not working, I mean—well, got to keep in condition, golf and tennis and the gym and well, *you know.*"

"Quit bragging," George said, "we all do that."

"Man and boy," Henry agreed. "Who wants more brandy?"

"Me," said Gordon.

"Me too," said George. He picked up a book and weighed it in his hand. "Books are too heavy these days. You need somebody to hold them for you."

"Too heavy for what's in them," Henry said.

Gordon twisted his head trying to read the title of the book George was holding. "*Bleak House,* is it?"

"I've turned to the nineteenth century," Henry said.

"Charles Dickens doesn't need royalties," Gordon protested.

"You still writing books?" George asked. "I thought you were working for us."

"I combine the two," Gordon answered, "business and business."

"I haven't read anything of yours lately," George said, "I only read synopses."

"That's all right, George, I don't see your pictures."

"Neither does anyone else," George said. "Business is lousy and we're not going to pay the crazy prices you boys have been getting."

"We always need good stories," Henry joined the conversation. "When we find them we'll pay for them."

"Say, George," Bobby interrupted, "do you think there's a chance of my picture playing the Music Hall?"

Gordon lowered his voice as he addressed Henry, "How is it possible that half the women in America think Duncan is so terrific?"

"Mine not to reason why," Henry said, "I just don't get it, there must be something lacking in the home life of American womanhood."

Gordon raised his glass, "To the nineteenth century and to dear, departed Dickens."

Henry sipped his brandy, "What George was saying is so, you know, the old boys did tell a story, a lot of story. They didn't linger for three hundred pages in someone's subconscious."

"Yes, but a lot of good stuff is being written, a lot of talented kids coming up. Anyhow I shouldn't be the boy to defend today's fiction. You may think I'm biased."

"Hell no, I don't mean your books. I'm on record as a fan." Henry passed him the bottle of brandy and went on talking. "There is some good stuff being written today, but most of it is thin or downright pornography."

"What do you mean by thin?"

"Bodiless, flimsy, too subtle; scene: the analyst's couch or the hussy's bed. Title: inevitably a line from Eliot."

"T.S.?"

"Certainly not George."

"What?" George Altman asked, turning around.

"Not you, a lady George," Henry said, "and I wonder where the girls are?"

"By the way," George Altman addressed Henry, lowering his voice so that it didn't carry to Gordon and Bob, "We've just signed a girl. I'd like you to look at her test tomorrow. Potentially great, she's got a lot of equipment but needs experience. I think it'd be smart to give her a little part in a big picture. Maybe in 'Rim of Heaven' there'll be something. I'd like to start her out right."

"What's her name?" Henry asked.

"Cindy Dobbs. That's her right name too. Cute. From Texas. Cindy Dobbs. Ever hear of her?"

"Yes," Henry said, smiling, "I think Sue has met her." Wait until Sue heard this. He laughed inwardly, observing that George was faintly startled.

Gordon stood by the fireplace, listening to the flames licking the coals in the grate. The *fine* warmed him as much as the fire. He savored its dark, golden taste.

He always enjoyed being in this house, he thought. A happy marriage is the most attractive thing a house can have; it is irresistible, people are drawn to it, like to be close to it.

He looked at the snapshot of Sue and Henry that stood on the mantel. *They're lucky and it's not wasted on them, they know it,* he reflected.

Gordon had liked Sue from the moment they had met,

but Louise hadn't . . . "There's something so unreticent about her," had been Louise's comment.

"She's happy and in love and I think she'll make Henry happy," Gordon had said.

"Possibly," Louise had said, looking superior, "but she seemed to have, I don't quite know how to say, she has no sense of sin."

"How the hell can you tell and what difference does that make?" Gordon had demanded. "Anyway I like her. I like her a lot."

And I always liked her, he thought, *and because of her, in a way, I have Alma . . . but have I? This obviously can't go on indefinitely, it wouldn't be fair to Alma. If she went to Europe with me that would only prolong it, make it tougher for her. No, it can't go on this way.*

There was a rustle in the doorway and the sweet, special scent of her perfume.

"Sue wants the men to come in and have coffee," Alma said. "The Rodgers are here."

The others went into the living room as Gordon turned from the fireplace and looked at her.

"I wish we were at home," she said.

"I could be more explicit," he said.

3

IN THE living room everyone was clustered around the Rodgers, hugging them and telling them how well they looked and asking questions about their trip all at the same time.

Sue poured coffee from the heavy, ornate silver pot into small white porcelain cups. George Altman sat beside her, yawning and blinking his eyes. "Good dinner," he said, "made me drowsy."

Gordon and Alma came into the room. "Coffee, Gordon?" Sue asked.

"One sugar, please."

"Gordon!" Luke Rodgers exclaimed, "I didn't know you were out here. We tried to get you in New York the other day."

They walked across the room, talking, to the piano.

"How well Gordon looks," Milly Rodgers remarked to Alma. "He's attractive, for a writer, don't you think?"

"Have some more coffee, Mil," Sue said before Alma had time to answer.

Isabel tapped George's knee. "Why don't you go in the other room and lie down? You're falling asleep."

"What a pretty dress!" Alma said to Milly.

"Rome," Milly said, "their copy of a Piguet, and for nothing. Millions of lire, of course, but nothing in real money."

"That's for me," said Isabel, "better than Paris, I hear."

"Unbelievable what you can get over there for an American dollar," Milly said. "Oh, Alma, I brought a present for you from Rome."

"Didn't you bring me anything?" Isabel demanded.

"It's not from me," Milly smiled archly, "it's from an old friend of Alma's."

"Alma is certainly a quiet worker," Isabel exclaimed.

"It's only from Ray Tavis," Alma said, "he wrote me

that Milly was bringing some things back for me. It was sweet of you, Milly."

Luke Rodgers seated himself at the piano and began to play a waltz.

"This is what you hear all over Paris. At Monseigneur they give it to you with ninety fiddles."

Gordon leaned against the piano and Jean fitted herself into the curve of the other side.

Alma wanted to go to the piano but somehow she couldn't, not with Jean standing there. Her dress really is cut indecently low, Alma thought. When she leans forward, as she was doing, you could see everything and Gordon was looking. At least he was not looking anywhere else.

Then Jean said something in a low voice to Gordon and began to dance alone to the music, holding out her arms toward him.

If he so much as touches her, Alma thought—then caught herself. She felt dizzy and embarrassed. *So this is part of it,* she thought, *part of being in love, being jealous. But Jean doesn't mean anything to Gordon, she couldn't, it's just that what Sue said frightened me.*

She slipped away from the group by the fireplace and stood at the foot of the stairs, wondering whether to go back to Sue's bedroom or into the garden. She had to cope with this new feeling, bring it out into the open as Dr. Loewy had urged her to do about any problem. If problem was the right word for this humiliating fear.

She opened the closet door to get her fur stole.

"Going somewhere?"

He was suddenly behind her.

She started. "I didn't hear you. I wanted some air. It's so warm in there. I thought no one noticed."

"I did," he said. "Come on." He opened the door and they went out of the house as they had come in, together.

CHAPTER SIX 　　*T*HEY walked like players in a pantomime, mute and purposeful, to the end of the garden. The fog had lifted and the moonlight fell like frosting on the wet, white flowers and the earth still glossy with damp.

At the end of the garden against the white brick wall and between two olive trees there was a white iron seat. Gordon brushed it with his handkerchief and Alma sat down. Now that they were alone again she felt shy and confused. Her resentment of Jean seemed trivial but the things that Sue had said remained. Even being alone with Gordon didn't banish them.

The white, gauzy light gave an aspect of unreality to the garden and to Alma. She seemed silvery and insubstantial as if there was another dimension between them. Gordon felt as if he were looking at a memory of her.

"You'll make a fine ghost," he said.

"And haunt you?"

"You haunt me now." He took her hand.

She drew her hand away and didn't reply.

"What's the matter?"

"Nothing."

"Tell me."

"I'm depressed. It'll go away."

"What's depressed you?"

"Thinking about your going away."

"I was thinking about that, too." His tone was grave.

"You mustn't feel guilty about it," she protested. "You know how happy I've been."

"You're not happy now."

"That's just for the moment."

He took a pack of cigarettes from his back pocket and offered her one. She shook her head and he lit a cigarette for himself. Then he spoke. "Let's talk about it."

"Not now. Let's just be together and be happy."

"It's not that simple." He tapped the ash from his cigarette. "I know this is a difficult situation for you. That's one of the reasons I wanted it to be kept quiet from Isabel and the other gossips. I didn't even want Sue to know."

"I don't care who knows," Alma burst out, "I only wish somebody would tell Jean Fielding."

"What's she got to do with it?"

"Nothing at all, forget it, Gordon."

"One reason for being quiet about it is Louise."

"I sometimes forget that you are married," she said.

"I'm afraid we both have to remember it."

Surprisingly, she laughed. "That's what Sue's been telling me."

"I see."

"I wonder if you do see," she asked sadly.

93

His cigarette had gone out and he lit another. In the brief flare of the match his face was set and stern. *It had to come,* she thought to herself, *but why now, why so soon?*

As if he'd read her thought, Gordon said, "This isn't the best time or place to discuss it. But it's been on my mind—" he thought of the wasted hours at the studio— "for quite a while."

"Yes, Gordon."

"I should never have allowed it to reach this point. I know more about these things than you do."

"Go on."

"If you think I'm selfish," he said, "you're right. And let me remind you that you knew I was married."

"But I thought it was the kind of marriage . . ." She looked at his face and couldn't finish the sentence.

"You don't know what kind of a marriage it is."

"You said that you hadn't really lived together in years," Alma attempted to explain. The jealous anger at him seemed to be disappearing. She wished that they could stop this and go home together. She looked at him entreatingly, but he wasn't looking at her.

"I've never really talked about my wife to you," he said, "or to anyone. But I'm going to."

Alma raised her hand involuntarily as if to ward off a blow. I wish I hadn't started this, she thought painfully. If we have such a talk we can never get back to the way it was. Then she listened to what Gordon was saying.

"I owe Louise a great deal. In the fifteen years we've been married and before she has been my friend. One of the few friends I've ever had; sometimes I've thought

94

the only one. I did say that we hadn't slept together for a long time, and maybe I made it sound more important than it is."

"Well, isn't that important?" Alma asked. "If it hasn't been your wife—then who . . . ?"

"Hell, I could sleep with a hundred women, I probably have. But I'm not going to leave my wife just because I go to bed with a girl."

It was brutal and he knew it. He stopped and looked at Alma. Her hands were folded in her lap and she was staring at him. He lit another cigarette and went on, "Louise usually hears about it, somebody tells her, or she divines it and we have a bad time, very bad. It's my fault. I like women. I like them a lot. Most men do. Most men are unfaithful to their wives, even if only mentally, when they look at a girl and wonder how it would be with her. I usually find out, and I used to find out even when Louise and I were still . . . when everything was all right with us; but that's beside the point. I don't say that my marriage is perfect, or even good, or the kind I would like to have had. As far as that goes, I didn't want any kind of a marriage, but Louise did. And I didn't want to lose her."

"I didn't know," Alma said quietly.

"Now you know," he said. "That's the way it is. We can go on while I'm here. I'd like that, Alma, but only if I know that you are quite sure what you're doing."

"Could I have a cigarette?" she asked.

"Of course," he opened a new pack. "Don't decide now."

Alma said, "You haven't said how you feel about me."

95

The smoke from their cigarettes hung in the air between them like a veil.

"You are the most beautiful girl I've ever known. I love going to bed with you. I wanted to the first time I saw you and I want to this minute. And now you really know how things are and it's up to you what happens."

There was a pause of what seemed like several minutes during which there was no sound from either of them. From the house for the first time they heard the distant, animated chatter of the party.

"It's cold," she shivered, "I'd like to go home."

"Shall we tell Sue you're not well or something?"

"I'll explain tomorrow. You don't need to come with me. I'll take Sue's car." She began to walk quickly toward the little gate in the wall and after an uncertain glance at the house, he followed her. They both reached his car at the same time and without a word they got in.

There was very little traffic on the road. Gordon wound down the window at his side and then wound it up. Alma sat in her corner as far from him as it was possible to get in the limited space and studied her handbag with rapt attention. He had an idea that she was trying hard not to cry but when he asked her if the door on her side was locked she replied that it was in a perfectly natural voice. He didn't say anything more, nor did she.

Gordon turned on the radio and instantly dance music played by a band in the ballroom of a San Francisco hotel filled the car as it drove rapidly along the wet asphalt of Wilshire Boulevard.

It was a good band and for the rest of his life Gordon

would not forget that they had played *Some Enchanted Evening, Time on my Hands, Jealousy* and *The Basin Street Blues* in that exact order.

When they began on *Basin Street* Alma said, "I detest that song."

Gordon switched to another station.

"Beethoven," he said. "The Fifth."

Alma couldn't help smiling. "Too bad Ray isn't here," she said, "he was nutty about it."

They reached her street. Gordon turned into the short driveway, switched off the radio but left the motor running. He got out of the car and went around to open the door for Alma.

She took the platinum key from her purse and gave it to him. He unlocked the door and held it open.

"Think about what I've said."

She nodded.

"I'll call you tomorrow." He gave her back the key and she went into the house. "Shall we have dinner tomorrow night anyway?"

"If you'd like."

He bent his head and kissed her lightly.

They hesitated, each wanting the other to say something more. The silence grew, dwindled. The moment passed.

"See you tomorrow then," he said with a heartiness that sounded absurd.

She lifted her face. It was very pale. "Good-night, Gordon."

He closed the door and went back to the car.

He sat in the car, not quite certain that he would be

able to drive. At times when he was greatly upset he seemed to lose his mechanical sense.

But he couldn't sit here in the car or go back into the house and say, "I've forgotten how to drive." He laughed at himself and put his hands on the steering wheel and at that second the lights went on in the house. That meant she was no longer standing in the hall. For another moment he watched the door, half-expecting it to open and Alma to come out, come running to the car, her long skirt billowing behind her and say, "It's all right, however you want it, Gordon. I can take care of myself. Come in with me."

And if she did, would he and would it be fair? She must have some time alone to think about them without his being there to confuse her.

She's grown up, Gordon argued to himself, *she's twenty-nine. She's been married and divorced. It's her life and she can do as she pleases. I've told her exactly how it is with me, which is more than I've ever done for anyone else. It's not my responsibility.*

He heard a voice, an echo of Louise saying during an old argument, "If anyone breaks her heart because of you, it will be your responsibility, Gordon."

"The hell it will," he said aloud. "Why do women love the word heart? They know perfectly well what it is they're talking about and it isn't the heart."

He backed the car out of the driveway and made a turn in the middle of the street.

A cloud blew across the white face of the moon. A handful of raindrops fell on the car. He turned on the windshield wiper and listened to its whining complaint all the way to the Bel Vista.

Room 119 was arranged for the evening. The night maid had been in to see to it. The curtains were drawn at the window, the ash trays emptied, one of the beds in the alcove turned down, the sheet folded back to a precise white triangle. Gordon switched on the light and to him the room had the unwelcoming air of any place where you hadn't expected to be and found your-self, suddenly and disappointingly.

Inviting as the morgue. He locked the door and slipped the night bolt as the sign on the wall requested. He thought of his earlier cheerful exit from this room after he had talked to Alma on the telephone. "You can take a shower here," she had said, "hurry up, darling."

He tossed the room key with its dangling brown tag onto the desk and took off his coat. There were drops of rain on the shoulders and he hung it over a chair to dry. *And I was feeling so good. Too good. Too good. Well, I took care of it. The end of a perfect day. Probably the end of Alma and me. I was subtle, too. Next to hitting her over the head with a bat I couldn't have done a better job.*

He sat down heavily in one chair and put his feet up on another, trying to make some sense out of what he had done. Why hadn't he waited until tomorow? Why ruin Alma's evening and leave the Calders' without even saying good-night? Sue would be cross. He would send flowers in the morning or something else; flowers were banal unless you were in love. Perhaps a pound of fresh caviar with a note to eat it all by herself with a spoon. She had once told him that was one of her ambitions.

He wrote *Sue caviar spoon* on one of the memo pads the hotel provided.

I would like to know, he thought, *exactly what my old friend Mrs. Calder said about me to Alma.* Whatever it was, it wasn't encouraging. Sue had probably been right, but it was easy to be right about other people's problems. Of course, he could have made it easier for Alma if he had told her about the child. But that was private, that was between Louise and himself.

Aware that he had a headache, he went into the bathroom to see if he had any aspirin. It was the first time since meeting Alma that he had been in the hotel at night by himself. Sometimes she came here with him but usually they had gone to her house.

"After all," Gordon had said to her, "the Bel Vista is a good hotel but it doesn't supply green silk sheets and an acre of mattress."

"And we don't have to be so quiet," Alma had said so seriously that he had laughed, "no one can hear us at my house."

He found a box of aspirin and swallowed two tablets but they stuck in his throat. He went back to the bedroom. It seemed cramped. However long you live in them, he thought, there is no sense of homecoming to hotels. His mind turned to the apartment in New York, the bookshelves, the windows that looked out on Sixtieth Street, the windows that looked out on the back yard next door, which had a fat little fountain, the typewriter that was built into the left-hand drawer of his desk, the only chair that he'd ever found that was comfortable for typing and the red-papered closet in the hall that they used as a bar.

And best of all, outside the door was New York. New York, he nearly cried out. If he was there he could be walking through the streets more alive and mysterious at midnight than at teeming noon. He thought of the summer nights when the pavement still held the unremitting heat of the day, when people slept in parks, slept on fire escapes, trading the city dweller's privacy for the chance of a breeze. Those scorching midsummer nights when the towers like grotesque parched throats strained toward the red-black starless sky.

Louise had once said about an unsuccessful short story of his, "Walk at night if you want to, Gordon, but let Thomas Wolfe write about it."

As usual her judgment was good, he thought. I love it too much to write about it well. Thomas Wolfe wasn't born there and I was.

"New York, New York, it's a hell of a town," he hummed, the refrain of one of his favorite songs about the city. I'm a simple man, he thought. I don't want to be carried back to ole Virginny, or that shanty in shantytown, or a little grass shack, or an old Kentucky home, or any place on earth for very long but New York. And now I am far away. Far, far away. If I was there I could stand being unhappy.

But, of course, I'm not really unhappy, he assured himself, pacing from bed to bureau. I'm concerned about the script, but everybody gets stuck once in a while, no need for panic to set in.

He poured some whiskey into a glass, hoping that it would have a sedative effect. He was tired, but not sleepy, a frequent paradox. The relentless energy of his nerves staved off sleep. But these days of struggling with

101

words that wouldn't come were more tiring than so-called hard labor. He knew that any man who had put in a day of such work, in the fields, the roads, the mines, would sneer at comparing the typewriter to their tools. But they'd be sound asleep by now. Work done with the body was kinder in that way than work with the brain.

It was imperative that he have a night of sleep before the meeting with Henry. He wanted it to be a productive meeting, because now more than ever he wanted to finish the script and return to his own work and his own city.

He put the cork back in the bottle. He'd better buy some more Scotch when he ordered the caviar for Sue at that fancy place on Beverly Drive.

A copy of the novel that he was adapting for the screen was on the desk and he picked it up. *Rim of Heaven*, the title jeered at him. Nearly four months and he wasn't finished yet. Three months of the four he had known Alma. If she was a reason for his inability to work well it certainly looked now as if that obstacle had been removed.

"Hell, I'm getting too old to develop a conscience." He stirred his drink with the end of a yellow pencil, "It doesn't agree with me."

Suppose he was never going to see her again. He considered this. Never again. Never hear her say his name in that soft unbelieving cry of delight (Gordon, Gordon, the two syllables became beautiful when she said them). Not awaken and know that she was beside him, curled against him, in her total, untroubled sleep. Never again. . . .

He began to take off his clothes, afraid that otherwise

he'd go out. It was raining in earnest now, no night for the aimless driving that he used to do before he had met Alma. Those drives had been useful; alone on the hard, fast roads he found that his mind settled to solving some of the questions the script raised. The work went better the next day for that preparation. It had been full of problems from the first, censorable angles and values that were difficult to transfer from one medium to another. "It's a tough one," Calder had said when they first discussed it on the telephone. "I really need you, Gordon. Read the book and let me know."

Odd, the things that affect a life, Gordon reflected. A man in London writes a book, another man in Hollywood reads it, and calls a third man in New York. If Mr. Standish had not written this work of fiction Mr. Cram probably would not be in Hollywood. Gordon raised his glass, "In your eye, Standish, old fruit."

If only he'd stayed at the Calders', or to be exact, if he hadn't gone into the garden with Alma, he thought, regretfully. It had been a pleasant party. Sue and Henry managed things well and it had been good to see Luke Rodgers again.

He sat down and looked at the Sunday Book Review of the New York *Times* which he had saved to read at a quiet time.

This was a quiet time. A little past midnight. He looked long at the cover photograph of Thomas Mann and wondered what Alma was doing. Taking off the lavender dress, brushing her hair, brushing her teeth, putting on one of her lacy nightgowns. Suppose he called just to say good-night. No, it was not a good idea. She might ask him to come over and he certainly would because he wanted to, there was no point in deceiving himself, "My God, how I want to. . . ."

He listened for a while to the sounds of nothing in particular. Plumbing rumbling in the walls, a quick tapping knock at an adjacent door. The rain. A fragment of conversation between two men walking in the corridor.

"You can take Canasta, Jack, I said to him, with you boys I play strictly Whist."

"Right, absolutely right. That Jack is a . . ." a door was closed.

Gordon went back to the reviews. There was one that interested him of a first novel which Louise had told him about before he left New York. Dover House had published it and she wanted him to read the galleys but he had forgotten until now. The review, by a well-known author, was not unfavorable but patronizing and made Gordon angry. "I'll ask Lou to send me the book."

He turned the page and there was a familiar face. Why, it was Eva Splane! So at last she had written the book she'd talked about incessantly and no one had believed she'd ever write. Gordon was amazed. He had known her for years; at one time Louise had liked her and they had seen her fairly often. She had come to New York from some place to write and to have many lovers. She'd always been asking Gordon's advice about both. She had bored him and he had never paid much attention to her until the war when he had been in London for a few weeks and found she was there, too. She had one of those nebulous jobs for which she wore a uniform and went to a great many cocktail parties, still chattering about her book—and now here it was. "I must buy

104

it," Gordon said, "and not ask Louise to send it. She'd suspect my interest and she'd be right."

He studied Eva's picture. She looked prettier and less intelligent than she was. Wise photographer, Gordon thought. If he liked the novel even moderately he'd write her a note. The last time he had seen her was when they met, by accident, on Fifth Avenue. She'd told him that she was taking a house in Connecticut and hoped that he'd come to visit. She'd been quite wistful, he remembered. It had been a cold day, before Christmas; her eyes were watering and her nose, never her best feature, was red. He hadn't liked the way she looked, clutching her parcels and sniffling and hinting for an invitation to tea or a drink. He'd decided that only the exigencies of war had made her seem passably attractive *or maybe I was won by the uniform*, he'd smiled to himself. He'd been quite rude to poor old Eva that day, he realized now. He'd definitely write her a note even if the book was awful. *The Heart's Reply*, terrible title. Women and hearts. It was an obsession with them.

He scanned the Books and Authors column, uninterested until he found his name: "Dover House is counting on a new novel as yet untitled from Gordon Cram for their fall list."

"Gordon Cram is counting on it, too," he said, "as yet untitled, as yet unfinished. Five chapters and a folder of notes in the file."

The idea of the unwritten novel for which he had already received a sizable advance combined with the dreary memory of Eva Splane added to his feeling of irritation at himself. He tore the book section in half and threw it into the wastebasket.

105

He poured some more Scotch. "The well known re-assurer!" he said to the tired yet healthy-looking man in the mirror.

It is deplorable the way I am wasting time tonight, he thought, drinking Scotch and lukewarm soda. There were many things he ought to do. Write to Hammond, his agent, about the offer from *Holiday* magazine. All the things that he didn't have time to do at the studio and that he hadn't done in the evenings because he had been with Alma. He thought again of how she had looked when he had left her in the hall of her house, so white and drawn and quiet. Was she one of the few women in the world who didn't privately enjoy scenes? What he used to call household histrionics.

Louise always insisted that she hated quarrels. But he knew that in some way they were necessary to her; that was why she provoked them, sometimes with reason, sometimes not. Of course, he must remember that Louise had very little else to do for emotional excitement.

There was something about sitting here that reminded him of the old, half-forgotten time after his mother had died. Not the surroundings, of course, nothing could less resemble the cheap apartment that he had lived in with his father. But the abandoned inner feeling, the sense of unnamed despair and loss was the same. Once before, waiting at the hospital with Louise, he had recognized this feeling of a lonely child within a grown man.

His thoughts turned, as they rarely did, to the years with his father. Every night they had prepared the evening meal together in the clean, dingy kitchen and eaten

106

it in silence. After dinner Gordon would carry the dishes to the cracked sink. He could still smell the decaying garbage in the corrugated can into which he emptied the remains of their food.

His father would sit in the living room reading the newspaper. Gordon would sit opposite him, the hard electric light shining on them condemned to each other for the eternity that had been Gordon's childhood. After a few minutes devoted to digestion and newsprint his father would turn on the radio and that would be the moment when Gordon could make up his stories, only pretending to listen to the radio. Some stories were entirely his own, others were his sequels to books he had read; either served to remove him from the room and the radio and his father and put him on a sailing ship in a high sea or with Washington at Valley Forge or on a farm feeding chickens or with Custer, the Indians approaching. The books became his reality, *Ivanhoe, Kidnapped, Stover at Yale*, all books, any books transformed him from Gordy, the boy whose mother was dead, to a boy living a rich and exciting life. He had had a bad time as a child, no doubt of it, but it had made him irretrievably into a reader and a writer. His father disapproved of both. He permitted Gordon to read at home for only an hour a day. When he won prizes in school . . . composition in the fifth grade, themes in the seventh, essays in the eighth, even though he was editor of the school monthly for the last three years of high school his father had been displeased. "Fit yourself for a job," was all that he'd said. "Don't waste time with words. You have to earn a living. I'm not going to support you."

Summer was difficult because there was no school and he couldn't write down the stories unless he went over to see his friend Joey Collins. There Mrs. Collins could be persuaded to let him sit in her parlor and write. "I don't know that it's natural, Gordy," she'd say, "but I don't suppose there's any harm to it."

Years later when his first novel was published he had gone uptown to see her and bring her a copy. She'd shown it to everyone, "Remember Gordy Cram, lived next door to us for years. Always was a smart one, had something in *The American Boy* when he was only a little feller. His mother died, God rest her soul, and his father was hard on the youngster. I remember the row when he wanted to go to college."

But I went to college anyway, Gordon thought, *in spite of that mean old bastard.* But he no longer felt the bitterness or anger, that was long past. He had defeated his father because he had done what he wanted to do. The old man had been proud of Gordon's success and the success had compensated for some of the hurt of the early years for Gordon. Before his father had died Gordon had come to realize that he was not an ogre but only a disappointed, undemonstrative man. Perhaps ogres exist only in the climate of childhood.

Louise had understood his father and helped Gordon to understand him. She was very young then, Gordon thought, but wise. She had been wise about his becoming a writer, and more than anyone else she was responsible for it. Louise had a small job in a publishing house. She, too, loved books and her family had teased her and discouraged her as a child but they stopped when she started to work at Dover House. When the first novel, which she had alternately scolded and encouraged him into writing, was written she herself took it to Will Tucker at Dover House, although she was extremely shy and greatly in awe of the famous editor. Will Tucker read it about two weeks later, sent for Gordon and arranged a contract and an advance. Gordon didn't believe that he could ever be as happy as he had been that afternoon. Neither would Louise, he supposed.

Louise had been (and still was) one of the few people he had ever been able to talk to about anything serious or important. With the girls before Louise he had made jokes and banter in the fashion of the day and when he kissed them he told them how pretty they were. With the boys he had exchanged dirty jokes and compared progress with the girls. But with Louise it was different. They talked about everything, both pleased and stimulated at finding someone who was interested, who understood. Although they never called it by that name, they had each experienced the same loneliness. Louise had been as lonely as he, not the loneliness of an only child but of a child alone in a large family. Not only in talk was she apart from the others; he had known from the first time he'd kissed her that he could do anything he liked with her. Though she never said so she made him feel that she belonged to him. He still saw other girls occasionally but only when he couldn't be with Louise, who was only allowed to go out with him three nights a week and not encouraged to "keep company" as her mother called it.

But what deepened and stabilized their relation more than anything else was the money he received from

Dover House. He stopped working for his father, moved out of the apartment and rented a room. Suddenly there was a place where they could be alone together. At first she had been surprisingly reluctant about taking the final step. She was in love with him but the scruples and prohibitions of her girlhood went deeper than they had thought in the days when there had been no place to prove it. He often wondered what would have happened if he hadn't rented the room. He might have met someone else—he had an immense zest and curiosity about women—but he was poor in those days and hard-working and Louise was enough. They had been happy. It had been in many ways the best period of their lives. The time without quarrels, the time when Louise hadn't been consumed by jealousy because she'd had no reason. When the book came out and was so successful he knew that Louise expected him to marry her and he felt that he had to. If it hadn't been for her *John Marriott* would never have been written and he'd still be working for his father and terribly unhappy. Besides she was the only person in the world whom he loved.

But there was no point in dwelling on the past, on Louise or his father or any of it. He had achieved success and acclaim by the standards of his time. By his own standards was he a success? Far from it. Despite the varying popularity of seven novels and innumerable short stories he still felt more than occasional doubt and discouragement. He thought reproachfully that he had yet to write a single page of which he was proud. When the war came he had fought in it, two years of infantry all over Europe; he had come out alive and not disgraced himself. He earned a large sum of money each year by his own efforts. He had two bank accounts. He had bought his wife a mink coat and a Matisse to hang over the mantel. He ate good food and drank good whiskey and people asked his opinions and read his books. His suits were made to his measure and his shirts and his shoes. He had started out being very poor and unknown and now he was a self-made success. *Self-made,* he smiled, *with the exception of a little help from Will Tucker and Louise Barnard.*

"I want to talk to you about my wife." He had said that to Alma in the garden. *I didn't handle it well,* he thought. He'd written that kind of scene several times and they'd been better than his levelling at Alma. Why? For being loving and innocent and unwise enough to wonder what would happen to her as a result of her life with him.

And I thought the old man was cold-blooded, Gordon laughed grimly, *Christ, I didn't have to be that hard on her.*

He put out his cigarette in the overflowing ash tray and emptied it thinking, *I've never talked about Louise to anyone. I guess I didn't have to, they knew what the score was, or perhaps I didn't care enough to tell them.*

He wished that the phrase "I love going to bed with you" would stop repeating itself in his head. He looked at the narrow bed and then at the telephone. It waited, black and bleak and silent yet as disturbing to a man as the mermaid's singing.

"I won't call her tonight. Not after the things I said, not after punishing her because I'm bound to a woman she's never seen by something she doesn't suspect."

I must be drunk or going crazy, he thought, *talking*

111

out loud. My God, what a foul evening I made from one that began so promisingly. I wind up at twelve-thirty in the morning drinking too much Scotch and remembering things I want to forget.

"How do you spend your spare time, Mr. Cram?"

"I feel terribly sorry for myself whenever I have a free moment because I've made one woman unhappy for fifteen years and it looks as if I'm letting another one in for the same thing."

He washed his face, brushed his teeth, set the alarm, turned out the lights and got into bed deciding not to read. *What will Alma say tomorrow night,* he wondered, lying in the dark waiting for sleep. He knew that she was in love with him and she was not a clever girl, yet the instinct for self-preservation is strong and performs remarkable rescues.

"Hell, what a mess," he declared to the dark room, expecting no answer and no answer came.

112

CHAPTER SEVEN *H*ENRY CALDER
bolted and locked the door as the last car drove away.
"Thought they'd never go," he said. "Good party,
Susie."

Sue paused as she emptied the ash trays. "I'm glad
it's over." She looked around the living room. "Isn't it
a mess?" she said happily.

"Let it go till the morning," Henry yawned. "Did I
drink too much?"

"Did you?"

"Yes."

"Come along then, darling. I'll get you an aspirin
and an alka-seltzer and you'll feel better."

"I feel fine," Henry said, as they went upstairs. "Say,
where the devil did Alma and Gordon go?"

"Guess."

"Couldn't they wait?" Henry asked. "Right after dinner, it'll impair their digestion."

113

"I've never heard that in my life," Sue said, "and I don't hold with it."

He laughed. "Little Miss Alma is certainly making up for time. Ray Tavis wouldn't believe it."

"Here's the alka-seltzer," Sue said, "and drink it down all at once, don't sip it like rare old port."

"Thank you," Henry said.

"I really could be cross at them," Sue said, stepping out of her dress. "Suppose I had needed them. The party went well from the start but they might have had some sense of social obligation."

"Would you take off my shoes, please? I get dizzy when I bend down."

Sue unlaced one shoe. "I'm afraid I rather upset Alma."

"Why?"

"Advice to the lovelorn." Sue began to unlace the other shoe. "I told her she was letting herself in for a run of 'Back Street.'"

"I'm sorry you didn't talk to Gordon. It might be a good idea if he got his personal life settled. Something's wrong with him."

"I can't believe it."

"He'll probably pull out of it," Henry stretched. "I feel wonderful and awful, too. Have you seen my pajamas, sugar?"

"Please don't call me sugar. That's what you used to call Jean."

"And any number of other girls," he grinned.

"What were you and Jean talking about all evening?"

"That's a silly question." He found his pajama coat

and shook it out. "We talked about little Jeanie Fielding and how she grew."

"How do you think she looked?" Sue asked.

"She always looks the same to me."

"Oh, I see," Sue said coldly.

"Don't be absurd," he said.

"Don't you be," she said, "that's all."

"It's been over for years," Henry said. "Why do you persist in digging up the past? It was before I knew you anyway. Open the window and let's get some sleep."

Sue opened the window and leaned out. "It's raining again."

"Glad to hear it," Henry said.

"That makes it cosy for Gordon and Alma. There's something about the rain when you're in love."

"Uh-huh," Henry said.

Sue stayed at the window, letting the damp night wind blow over her bare arms.

"Do you think Gordon is in love with Alma?" she asked.

But Henry, already asleep, began to snore softly.

Sue thought about the women who had been up here tonight in their pretty dresses, powdered and perfumed, all with their problems locked inside them, as much a part of them as the hair on their heads. They had talked about cooks and mascara and liquid diets and pantie-girdles but, with the exception of Alma, not one of them, including Sue herself, had spoken about a thing that was really important. *Which is just as well*, Sue thought, *after all, it was a dinner party, not a revival meeting.*

Poor little Peggy Duncan, she was too young and too

inexperienced to deal with a man like Bob. Now Jean, with enough experience to handle any man, had no one to practice on. But that was only temporary; there were always men for Jean but all the same she looked lonely and tired and Sue had for one moment felt sorry for her. *Does she envy me?* Sue wondered. *Is she sorry she didn't marry Henry when she had the chance?*

If Jean did envy her she was right. Sue knew she had a good life and everything in it that she wanted, Henry and the children and her house and her friends. Still Jean had had her fun and would have more. If it was Jean with Gordon, Sue wouldn't worry. Jean had been hurt, as she was always the first to say, but she was tough in a way that Sue admired. Jean would always pick herself up and get going. But Alma, Alma was lost, drowned, dazed with love . . . What a look there was on her face when Sue had talked about Louise Cram!

Why didn't I keep quiet?

Now she watched the rain falling on her garden. *I must tell Jim to tie up the bougainvillaea.*

Strange how attached she was to the garden—she'd never thought of herself as a woman of the soil. "I hate nature," she used to say. "I like flowers that come in white boxes with a loving message on the card and plenty of that glazed green paper that smells wet." And now she had turned into a woman who read seed catalogues and, wearing heavy gloves, kneeled with a basket and real tools to work in the soft, rich earth.

Sue watched the dark branches blowing against the dark sky, so many shades of darkness that the room behind her lit only by the bedside lamp seemed glaringly bright as she turned back to it.

116

Absently, distractedly, she picked up her gray dress and slippers and put them away. If only Alma knew more about men, she thought, or if only Gordon knew less about women. But what good would that do? She unclasped her pearls and took off her earrings, replacing them in her jewel case.

Perhaps I've been unfair to Gordon, Sue mused. *What would he think if Alma repeats all the things I've said?* Who could ever really know Gordon's thoughts? He was impassive, implacable; with all his warmth, his wit, his easy friendly laughter, there was still his detachment, even, Sue supposed, in love. Of course Alma didn't think so but Alma was mad about him. *Literally mad,* Sue said to herself. She closed the closet door, snapped off the light, listened to the whine of the wind.

Should I have told her about the child, her thoughts continued, *that's really what's troubling me. But I couldn't tonight. Besides, it's not my story to tell. And I've told her quite enough about Gordon; in fact, too much.*

The rain was growing louder and wilder. Sue decided to close the window entirely. She drew the curtain, sighing, as she remembered Alma's face.

Henry snored so loudly that he woke himself up.

"Susie," he reached sleepily in the direction of her pillow.

"If you are looking for me, I'm not there," she said. "I'm here, taking the evening air."

"Come to bed, it must be late."

"I'm upset about Gordon and Alma," she sat on the bed. "I have such a peculiar feeling about them all of a sudden."

117

"Please, honey, it's after two," he said, "whatever it is, it will keep and so will they."

"It must be a delicious feeling though, to be in love with someone, passionately in love and alone without children or household problems, just being alone with someone you're crazy about, it must be wonderful."

"I'm sorry," said Henry, "that I love you as a friend."

"Damn it," she said as she got into bed.

"Don't get violent about it," he said, "you'll wake the children."

"Not that. I forgot to give you the aspirin."

"Never mind," he said, "just let me go to sleep."

"Good night, then."

"Good night, Susie," he said, "I really love you very much and not at all as a friend."

"And I'm glad that I've got you," Sue said, plumping her pillows, "even if it is all grown-up and settled down."

"If you really mean that," Henry said, "don't take all the blanket."

2

GORDON had fallen into an uneasy sleep, filled with half-dreams that skimmed and shifted, shadowy, formless, through his tired mind. And then he dreamed that he was in a tunnel, endless and slimy and then irrationally he was out of the tunnel and on the street that was the usual scene of his recurrent nightmare.

In this dream he was seven years old, roller-skating down the block with his friend Joey Collins who lived next door. Someone was calling his name, "Gordy, Gordy," and he saw his mother at the window calling down to him. In the dream he could never see her face but he heard her voice clearly, "Here, son," she would say, and then a little metallic clang as the coin hit the sidewalk, "You treat Joey." He was happy at that point of the dream and then as he went to pick up the coin— it never varied—she always said, "You treat Joey," and he would hear the scream, a long single note that shivered shrill on the air.

He woke up, damp with sweat, rigid with terror, still feeling hands pulling at his shaking, fighting, seven-year-old shoulders. He lay half awake in the dark, breathing through his mouth, his fists against his eyes to blot out the scene while the blood behind his eyeballs made frenetic patterns in the clotted darkness between the dream and the moment of release.

"Jesus," he whispered, "Jesus Christ."

He turned the pillow over and pressed his cheek against the cool side. He was now at the point of being aware that he had had a nightmare and wondering as he always did what caused it. He hadn't had it for several months, since before he had left New York.

He thought of getting up, getting dressed and getting out. But he remained in bed, still not quite out of the nightmare. *Is it because I was talking about Louise that I had it again tonight?* he asked himself. *Is it because I should have told Alma about the child?*

Despite himself, he recalled the beginning of it all. It had been a Saturday afternoon in the spring and he and Louise had been on their way to lunch, a late lunch to celebrate the sale of a short story. Those were the days when each sale called for a celebration.

They had been living for three years in an apartment in the brownstone house to which they had moved after their marriage. They had a small walk-up flat with a skylight in the bathroom. It was during the morning that Louise had said, "The people in the garden apartment have moved out. Would you like to look at it since it's available?"

"Let's see it," Gordon had said.

He knew that the garden apartment was a duplex and it was an idea that he'd always liked, a little house of their own. He was feeling affluent and successful with the big check in his pocket for the little story.

The garden apartment, they both agreed, was delightful. There was a small curving staircase, wood-burning fireplaces and a bay window in the living room.

"It's a lot more money," Louise had pointed out.

"And more rooms than we need, but I could use the back one as an office."

Louise had said quietly, "Or it could be the baby's room."

"One of these days, perhaps."

She went to the window and looked out at the back yard. "Would you mind so terribly?"

He looked at her then; she was standing by the unwashed, uncurtained window. Behind her in the yard was a naked plane tree and through its branches the afternoon light fell on her, wan and milky.

"How long?"

"Four months."

"You waited," he said, "until it was too late to do

anything about it." His voice sounded loud through the bare, untenanted rooms.

Louise didn't move or speak but her face, the attitude of her body, were a tacit entreaty.

"I was wrong not to tell you about it. But when the doctor said I was pregnant I thought why not, why not now, we are both doing well and I can keep working for a few more months and I thought if we had it you'd change your mind." Her voice trailed off.

"All right, Lou," he said quietly, "there's no point in saying any more about it."

"Then I may have it?"

"You seem to have made that decision by yourself." He tried to speak lightly. "Tell the agent we'll take this apartment. I imagine they'll paint it for us, but tell them we'll stay upstairs until they get this in shape."

She put out her hand. "Can you be happy about the baby?"

Taking the hand, he had squeezed it. "I'll get used to the idea," he'd said. "You'd better take it easy, darling, I'll be back in an hour or so. See you later."

And he had walked out of the apartment that they were to live in for so many years, leaving her standing in the rounded window. It wasn't until some time later that afternoon that he recalled they had been on their way out to a gala lunch.

The months that remained of her pregnancy he counted among the slowest and most unpleasant of his life. Worse even than the gloomy, struggling days of his childhood when he had been left alone with his father, missing friends and human warmth and laughter, with only the awful tinted photograph of his mother standing gilt-framed on the radio, a dead face that seemed never to have been alive. He would look at it for a long time when he was a little boy, trying to remember her, trying to love her, but there was only the posed permanent smile of the cerise lips. All he could remember was that he'd been playing in the street when she'd called to him. Then, still standing at the window, she had suddenly started to scream in agony and soon after the ambulance screamed down the street. They'd carried her downstairs on a stretcher, still screaming, and he remembered that the men had sweated carrying her even though she was so small.

Joey's mother, Mrs. Collins, had taken him for several days; she'd told him that he was going to have a little baby sister, wouldn't that be grand? It was fun staying at the Collins', thinking about the sister. He had almost forgot about the scream and being scared by it when one day, not long after he came in from school with Joey, he found Mrs. Collins sitting in the kitchen crying. She told Joey to go in the other room and put Gordon on her lap. Still crying, she had told him, "Your mother has gone to heaven, Gordy lamb. Do you understand, you poor little man?"

"When will she come back? Why did she go anyway? Did those men take her?"

Then his father had come in, his face closed. He thanked Mrs. Collins and had Gordon thank her and they went back to their own apartment.

"She's dead," his father had said. "She is not coming back ever. She's dead."

His mother was dead. His mother was dead. His mother was dead.

During the months that Louise was pregnant Gordon had thought again of that time of aloneness with his father and dreamed the old dream from which he'd awaken with the scream still sounding in his ears. And when he awakened he'd find Louise sleepless in the dark.

"Can I get you something, Loulie?"

"No, dear, thank you. You're so sweet."

He'd get out of bed and go into the other room for a cigarette because the smell of the smoke made her sick these days. He'd feel sick himself with pity and disgust. Pity and disgust were the only emotions toward her he seemed to be capable of in that time. The summer in New York was especially and destroyingly hot that year.

"I think you should get out of this heat."

"You want to get rid of me; I'm so hideous and you can't forgive me?" she'd say and begin to cry.

"That isn't it at all, darling. You'll be more comfortable out of the city."

At last in August she was persuaded to go to Maine. He took her to the train hoping he didn't show the embarrassment he felt when people glanced at her moving heavily beside him.

How un-private it is, he'd thought, buying peppermints and magazines for her at the newsstand in Grand Central Station.

She sits there as if she'd been planted, he'd thought walking toward the bench where she sat, her legs apart, her mouth open, panting a little amid the heat and activity of the station, her hands on the grotesque belly.

It's nature, he said to himself, *it's life, growth, fertility and, Jesus, it's ugly.*

"Time to go, dear," he said, helping her as slowly, awkwardly she got to her feet and they went to the train.

That summer had also been the time when—though he had always liked women and had a frankly sensual feeling about the attractive ones—he now found them more disturbing, more delightful than ever before.

He had a sudden, rather violent affair with a dancer called La Flamme who was working in a show at one of those roof-gardens that open in New York in the summer. He'd sit on her bed watching her dress, observing the liquid lovely line from breast to hip, from thigh to ankle, knowing rapture at the mere sight of her high breasts, the taut skin of her flat, hard stomach.

After Labor Day Louise returned from Maine and the roof-garden closed. La Flamme went to Chicago to dance in a nightclub there and Gordon never saw her again. Every part of Louise now seemed to have changed, her face, her feet, her arms were distorted and swollen. He couldn't remember how she had looked before.

As they waited for the final month to arrive he had none of those stirrings of pride and pleasure that fathers are supposed to experience. *Was it because he had not wanted a child,* he asked himself, *was it another form of his selfishness, or was it because of his mother? But nothing like that would happen to Louise,* he told himself. He waited with a patience that was new to him.

The baby was late, first a few days, then a week, then ten days. Louise, who had always been in such a hurry for everything, was undisturbed, uncomplaining about

124

the delay, although it was evident that she did not feel well.

"Doctor says it's hard to judge with first babies," she'd said to Gordon in the placid, bovine manner she had acquired in the last few months.

When the baby was a fortnight overdue the doctor said that Louise must go to the hospital. She had come into the room where Gordon was working and told him.

"I'm ready," she said, "I've been ready for two weeks."

"I'll get a taxi," he'd said, putting on his coat. "You're not frightened, are you?"

"Of course not," she'd smiled, "except about the castor oil they're going to give me, that'll be horrid."

He remembered standing on the corner of Sixtieth Street for what seemed a long time whistling at cabs . . . green, yellow, checkered . . . At last one stopped at the opposite corner to unload a passenger and Gordon hailed it.

Louise was waiting in the vestibule, holding her little overnight case.

He gave the taxi-driver the address of the hospital and pulled out the jump seat for Louise's feet. They held hands for the short ride. It was growing dark, the street lamps were on, the shop windows illuminated. They drove down Madison Avenue and Louise looked long-ingly out of the window. Then they were there.

He kissed her, he was no longer embarrassed, but he didn't want her to leave him; and he could see now that she was frightened. He wanted to tell her something, anything, that would reassure her, that would let her know that it was all right with him, but before he had a chance a nurse appeared, starched and aloof, to lead

125

her away down a long hall that smelled of ether and antiseptic and bedpans.

They told him to wait. He waited in a room at the end of a hall. He read magazines, did crossword puzzles and just waited, watching the hands of the clock. And all the while he heard the echo of that long-ago scream.

He waited for twenty-six hours in the execrable room. He smoked cigarettes, he dozed sitting up in the stiff wicker chair, someone brought him a ham sandwich which he ate. He drank much tepid, yellow coffee out of cardboard containers from the drugstore. He smelled the smells and listened to the bells and watched the lights that signaled the doctors and felt that he was waiting for his doom to be announced as he watched the clock in the way a prisoner watches his judge on the bench.

Then the doctor was standing in the doorway. His face was void of any expression but acute fatigue.

"Mr. Cram, I'm afraid I . . ."

"My wife?" Gordon interrupted, getting to his feet.

"Your wife will be all right, though she's had a bad time."

"Is the child dead?" Gordon made his voice low and level. He looked right at the doctor.

"Not dead," the doctor said. There was a long pause.

"What is it, doctor?"

"Sorry, these cases are difficult for everyone," the doctor said, drawing a hand over his face. "As you know your wife has not had an easy pregnancy for reasons not altogether physical. Her labor has been strenuous and we couldn't help her as much as we wanted to . . ."

"Please," Gordon cut in, "what's wrong?"

126

The doctor's voice went on as if by rote, "The thing to bear in mind in these cases is that it isn't anyone's fault, no one should have a sense of guilt. We don't understand these things, science, research, genes, but still we are largely in the dark. Many children are born subnormal, but in time we see changes for the good."

"Subnormal?"

"On the basis of what we find at this time the little boy is not normal, and will not progress normally."

"What exactly is wrong?"

"He is a Mongoloid," the doctor said.

"Do you mean a Mongoloid idiot?"

"We can't determine the degree at this early stage, and this is a tentative diagnosis, of course. Perhaps you'd like to consult another man."

"Could you be mistaken about it?" Gordon asked.

"There can be no mistake about a Mongoloid, unfortunately."

Gordon waited for a moment to answer. "Then there doesn't seem any point in consulting someone else, does there?"

"No," the doctor answered, "we have to be truthful, brutally truthful, or people go on from doctor to doctor, from place to place, hoping to hear that their child will be all right."

"Will it live?"

"I'm afraid so. He weighs seven pounds, five ounces."

"May I see it?"

"Of course. We usually don't tell the mothers until they are stronger. It's hard for the mothers, they always have a terrible guilt, all of them."

"I suppose so," Gordon said aloud but inwardly he

127

was repeating to himself endlessly, *Christ almighty, Christ almighty!*

He followed the doctor down the corridor.

"They can be sweet children," the doctor was saying, "and they require a great deal of attention and care. They are backwards mentally but they still yearn for affection."

"Are there places where . . . ?"

"There are many excellent places, rather like schools, you know, in the country."

"Do they die?"

"Before they grow up?"

"Yes," Gordon said, "before they grow up."

"In most cases at about the age of fifteen. Come this way."

They were in a little room which was hot, the stuffy, moist heat of a greenhouse. A nurse came in through another door. She held the baby, wrapped in a faded blue blanket. She drew aside a fold of the blanket and Gordon told himself to look. The head was large, rather misshapen; the face looked small under the protruding forehead. The eyes were shut but slanted. The whole face was wrinkled and purple as a prune. Gordon looked away to the miniature, perfect hand, the beautiful tiny fingernails. He touched the little fist.

"The tiny feet," the nurse said softly, undoing the blanket, "the feet are so cute." She sounded as if she were going to cry.

Gordon was conscious of a pain somewhere and of the excessive heat of the room.

"As there are no other children at present the adjustment will be easier for Mrs. Cram. This thing isn't inherited. I hope you understand that, Mr. Cram. I had another case last month. The father is a doctor and they have two other children who are perfectly normal. It's terribly bad luck. I'm very sorry."

"Thanks, doctor," Gordon said. "May I see my wife, now?" Inside of him, despite what the doctor said, he felt a mounting sense of his own vague responsibility for this outcome.

They went down in the elevator to Louise's room. There was a sign on the door that said NO VISITORS. The room was dim; there was one lamp lit on the dresser over which the nurse pinned a cone of paper so that there was almost no light. She drew a chair near the bed and Gordon sat down. The doctor handed him a paper cup. "Drink it," the doctor said. Gordon tasted it; it was whiskey. He thanked the doctor and he meant it.

"She'll come out of it soon," the doctor said, going to the bed. Then, seeking other words but not finding them, he left and the nurse tiptoed after him, holding the chart. The door closed noiselessly behind them. He was alone with Louise.

He looked around the cell-like, aseptic room, white walls, white iron bed, a few tired blue flowers in a vase.

Her face was a blur against the pillow, but the shape of her body was discernible under the counterpane. It had shrunken and flattened. Where, he wondered, had all that fat gone to. He thought of the blue blanket. Seven pounds, five ounces. It wasn't large. The tiny hand. He tried not to think of the head but when he thought of the hand with its little fingernails, he had a dull pain again under his ribs. It was a pain of loss, of losing something he had never had. He felt sick.

"Loulie," he whispered, "darling. Louise."

But she continued her exhausted sleep. For nine months she had slept fitfully and now she was sleeping deeply and undisturbed. She was breathing heavily but Gordon decided that it was from the drugs they had given her and from being so tired. She had had a bad time, the doctor said, she had suffered and they hadn't been able to help her and for what? He sat, not done with waiting, listening to the strenuous breath, waiting for her to wake up so that he could tell her what he felt she already knew.

Now he sat up in bed, wide awake, his thoughts with the pitiful child, who would be eleven in October, at this moment going through his purposeless routine at a retreat for such children in Connecticut. The albatross.

CHAPTER EIGHT $\mathcal{G}$ORDON was at the studio before nine o'clock. He walked down the long corridor still redolent of its early-morning soaping to Henry's office. The building had an empty feeling. Executives did not follow the stern hours of work imposed upon the help. Gordon wanted to find out from Rhea Brown if she knew what time Henry planned to have their meeting. But she was not at her desk.

The door to Henry's office was open and Gordon went in looking for Rhea. Seeing it as he rarely did, quite empty of people, Gordon thought what a pleasant room it was. It had an air of permanence in contrast to his own office on the floor above. Henry had said last night, "Nothing, no one is permanent out here. This business is built on a foundation as firm as jello."

From the huge window that took up most of one wall Gordon could see the studio below and the bald, brown mountains beyond. He watched the small figures of people going in and coming out of the big stages. To him it looked flourishing and imperishable, whatever Henry might think.

All around the room there were waist-high bookshelves; two shelves contained red leather-bound scripts of the dozens of pictures that Henry had produced. On the walls above hung framed stills from the successful ones.

What a lot he's made with Jean Fielding, Gordon thought, glancing at the walls. That arresting face with the oversized eyes and mouth, the hollows under the high, sharp cheekbones. . . . She had changed very little through the years; only the costumes and the make-up dated. Henry had commented about it to Gordon the other day, "She's a smart one. She knows there's no substitute for glamour, so she works to look like an actress. Not like some of those that run around looking messy, not even wearing lipstick. And she always knows her lines. There's no substitute for that, either."

She looked like a fan magazine's idea of an actress last night, Gordon grinned to himself, *that dress was the next barest thing to a French bathing suit.*

He left Henry's office and walked up a flight of stairs to his own. Luke Rodgers had mentioned last night that he had been assigned the office next door. Gordon looked in as he passed.

"Luke?"

"Hello." Luke was lying on the sofa. "Why the hell did you disappear last night?"

Gordon ignored the question and asked, "What's the matter with you?"

"We played the Game," Luke intoned, closing his

132

eyes. "Our team was lousy. We had the two actors, Fielding and Duncan and, believe me, they need a director. Whenever we play the Game out here the actors are the only ones who can't act. I hurt my back doing 'The Fall of the House of Usher.'"

"I knew charades were dull but I never knew that they were dangerous. Anyway I gave up parlor games when Spin the Bottle went out of fashion."

"Kissing games can be dangerous, that's how I met my first wife."

"I didn't sleep very well, Luke. Got any benzedrine?"

"Center drawer, the little bottle. See?"

"Thanks, very neighborly of you. Glad you're back, but I'd better get started."

"Don't be too hearty about it. Give it to them good but give it to them slowly, that's my motto."

"Sleep well," Gordon said, closing the door softly.

Marjorie Sawyer was not in yet. Gordon poured himself a glass of water and swallowed the pill.

On his desk there was a fresh copy of the script in its latest version from the stenographic department. It had canary yellow covers with the words 'Temporary Incomplete' stamped on the front.

"How true," said Gordon.

It seemed impossible that he would ever be through with it; that the writing, the thinking, the rewriting, the story conferences, the eternal bogging down and wrangling over a plot point or a line of dialogue or a joke, would ever be over. But one day, he supposed, the picture would be made and if he was here he'd go to the preview with Henry. They'd drive to Pomona or Inglewood or Santa Barbara in one of the big black studio cars that looked as if they also did double duty for an undertaker. They'd eat the sandwiches Sue had packed for them because Henry would be too nervous to sit in a restaurant and Henry's preview nerves were contagious. Then they'd meet the manager of the theater who, whether tall or short, fat or thin, always had the same face, the doleful, sadly smiling face of a man who understood their anxieties. Then they'd take their seats, watch the newsreel and breathe the stagnant candied air. Henry would wince at the sound of paper bags rustling, of teeth crushing crackerjacks, and especially of children crying.

A deadly silent card on the screen would announce, "Ladies and Gentlemen, this is a Major Studio Preview." Then music and the title 'Rim of Heaven' would follow on the screen and the interminable credits accompanied by scattered applause. Screen Play by Gordon Cram based on the novel by V. F. Standish. Produced by Henry Calder, with extra loud music over that one. Directed by Edward R. Doremus. And then the picture would begin and would at last be over. They'd wait for the cards that some of the audience filled in, expressing their opinions. They'd read them in the car driving back to Hollywood. They'd discuss what had played well, what hadn't, the awful laughs in the wrong places, the blessed laughs in the right places, the expression on George Altman's face as he left the theater. No thermometer ever performed its function more accurately than George's face on these occasions. When the picture was a real stinker he mercifully spared them ever having to see his face at all by dashing out a side door before

The End title had finished and disappearing alone into the orange-scented night.

Gordon turned the pages of the script, skimming the lines at random. There was plenty to do still ahead. He wondered if Eddie Doremus was going to direct *Rim of Heaven*. Henry had said, "Ed has a commitment with Metro, but if we can wait he'll do it."

"He'd be my choice," Gordon had said.

"Mine too," Henry had agreed. "He over-shoots and he's angle-crazy, but he's a great camera pointer."

Gordon laughed at that, "You always say that about Doremus and 'Cram writes good answers' about me."

"He is and you do," Henry had said, "you just don't write them often enough."

Gordon uncovered the typewriter and fed two sheets of blue paper into the machine. "Go on, go to work," he said to himself, "write some answers."

He typed for a while but his thoughts would not stay with it and the benzedrine was taking its time. He had a jittery feeling about Alma and wished it were settled one way or the other. It was a new and nervous feeling for him. He'd said that he would call her but he never had until the working day was over and that was hours away. He wondered where to take her for dinner. What would she say? She had probably had a difficult night making a decision. After all, she had so often said exultingly that he had changed her. Well, whatever her decision was, he would tell her that he realized last night that it had changed him too. What man in the world wouldn't be affected by having that power over a woman? Those things worked two ways, he discovered, a possession and a belonging.

He thought of a talk they had had last Sunday driving to the beach for dinner.

"I never understood what people were talking about or why it was so important," Alma had said, "but now I do, and I see how difficult it was for Ray. Perhaps if I'd known you first . . ."

"Maybe it never is right with some people, Alma, however much they'd like it to be."

"Why is it for us?" she'd asked.

"I don't know, baby, there are no blueprints. But if we don't stop talking about it there's going to be a nasty accident on Highway 101."

Was it any wonder, he asked himself now, that he had lost his detachment with Alma, the detachment that had let him keep his relation with the others on a simple unemotional level. All of them, Page, La Flamme, Laura Davis. They had left or he had left and it was over. But Alma was different. One of the main differences being that she was inexperienced and they were not. They knew the rules and she didn't. They were willing to go along for the ride but Alma had fallen in love with him, and he . . .

"Well, aren't you the early scholar!" Marge Sawyer said as she opened the door. He jumped.

"Sorry, didn't mean to startle you," she said. "Another day of glorious smog. How are you?"

"Cloudy and cold like the weather. Send for some coffee, will you, Margie?"

The telephone rang and it was Henry. He had to postpone the conference because an Altman uncle had arrived from the New York office and George Altman had called an economy meeting of all the producers.

136

"What about lunch?" Gordon asked.

"I'm lunching with a fellow from *Time*. Come along."

"I'll cramp your style," Gordon said, "you'll be talking about the future of the industry and I hate popcorn."

"Let's meet at two in my office then," Henry suggested. "Sorry you left so early last night. We had fun."

"I know," Gordon said, "I've seen Luke."

Gordon replaced the telephone and thought about calling her. But she'd still be asleep, curled in the center of her big bed looking very small. . . .

"This is going to be a great day, a very productive day," he said gloomily, snapping the page out of the typewriter.

2

WHEN he looked at the clock again the hands were at 12:30 and he had written a page and a half of dialogue that, to his surprise, he liked.

He opened the door. "Time to eat," he said to Marge.

"I'll wait till you get back," she said, "I'm on a diet, anyway."

He noticed the gardenia pinned to her jacket. "You happy, Marjorie?"

"I have a fella," she said, touching the flower lightly, "makes all the difference."

"So they tell me. Don't diet too much, you'll need your strength."

He looked into Luke Rodgers' office but it was empty.

He walked from the New Building in the direction of the commissary. The air was at once raw and oppressive and the people that he passed looked troubled and peevish. Personal problems, he wondered, or the prevailing mood of days lived under the invisible hovering shadow cast by a mushroom-shaped cloud?

"Watch out there or you'll get run over."

He was in front of a long chrome-yellow car, its canvas top down in defiance of the weather. Jean Fielding was driving it.

"Want a lift?"

"Sure," he said, "why walk when you can ride?"

"Where to?"

"The commissary, please, where the poor folks eat. Are you on your way to lunch in your dressing room?"

"Not today, I have to be in Wardrobe at one o'clock. Big crisis. Henry doesn't like the suit I wear in the last sequence."

"Have a sandwich with me?" Gordon suggested, looking at his watch, "you have time."

"Oh, I wish I could, but I promised I'd stop at the fan-mail department. I thought we'd have a chance to talk last night but you vanished."

"I'm sorry," he said, "and sorry about the sandwich." He opened the car door.

"I'd love to see you. Why don't you come down to the set this afternoon? Stage nine."

Gordon said solemnly, "I am not a proud man. I will do almost anything, but the one thing I will never do in this life is to sit on a set."

"Why?" Jean smiled, the slow, small smile that melted into the candid look. "We could talk."

"That is exactly what we could not do," he leaned against the car, "all those people, electricians, grips, painters, property boys, the extras playing gin-rummy. Your hairdresser, the make-up man for your face, the make-up man for your hands, the body make-up man. Your secretary, your maid, the girl who plays your phonograph records and all the visitors. The refugees with accents that tell you how much better they did it at U.F.A. twenty years ago and the cheese convention from Wisconsin that the publicity boys bring over to be photographed with you. I took a vow three years ago never to visit a set again. Some things are sacred to a man, things he just wouldn't do, like molesting minors, or drinking corn whiskey, or beating a woman on Sunday. Me, I don't visit sets."

Jean pouted. There were those who said that her pout was as powerful as her smile. "It's a pity," she said, "we never see each other and here we are at the same studio . . ."

"I just work here," he said.

"I have an idea. I'll be in Women's Wardrobe in fifteen minutes, why not meet me there?"

He hesitated. She laughed.

"You'll be chaperoned; my producer will be present."

"Henry told me he had a lunch date."

"He did. This came up after he ran the clothes tests this morning," Jean explained. "He says the suit's a dog. I said so at the time, but let's test it anyway, they said, and the outfit is supposed to work on Monday. I may kill that little louse Devon, what he doesn't know about clothes."

"I'll have a cup of coffee and meet you there."

"Devon's studio in fifteen minutes," and she drove off.

Devon might have been his first name or his last but it was the only one he used. He designed costumes only for the important women stars at R.A.M. but supervised the entire wardrobe department. No one seemed to be around when Gordon arrived but he saw a double door partly open at the end of the hall. He looked into a large, high-ceilinged room with pale rose walls on which an occasional silver flower was stenciled. At one end of the room there was a small stage flanked by huge mirrors and lit with an overhanging bank of shielded lights.

Henry Calder was sitting on the step of the stage wearing his glasses and an angry expression that indicated he had had no lunch and was hungry.

"Pardon me," said Gordon, "I was looking for the men's room."

"Spare me the humor," Henry said. "I met Jean. She told me you were coming. I didn't know you were a fashion authority, my boy."

"I'm versatile." Gordon looked around the room. "Quite a set-up this."

"It's a soft life if you can sew a fine seam," Henry said. "Take a chair."

Gordon sat on a red velvet ottoman and said, "I suppose we'll wait a while. These lady stars never learn to tell time."

"That's not true of Jean. She has her faults but she's a professional," Henry said. "There are two kinds: the ones like Jean who work hard, are never late on the set, don't believe that they can produce and direct and write the picture. They take care of themselves while they're shooting, don't go to Mexico and forget to come back or even tell the studio they're going. They're amiable about making tests, don't drink in their dressing-rooms or lay the cameraman between takes. They have talent and respect for talent, that's why they get where they are and stay there."

Gordon listened, interested. He had never heard Henry sound off like this before.

"You mean to say that all those with talent behave themselves that well?" he asked.

Henry thought this over. "Not the neurotics," he went on, "not the half-demented, maladjusted females found in beauty contests or a soda fountain who ring the bell because they have a sex-appeal that ticks and a vague instinct for acting. Their lives are so confused, their own doubt of themselves is so agitating, that they behave like the ego-maniacs they are. They're a curse to everyone who works with them. Always late, always mean, always unpredictable. Jean isn't like that."

"And how about the ones with no talent who raise hell?" Gordon asked. "How about those? There are plenty of them."

"Yes, you mean like Sherry Laine for instance, Coral Martin, beautiful girls, but what do they do with their chance?—they behave badly, fight with everyone, give themselves airs, won't pose for pictures, won't give interviews, won't work on Tuesdays or some such nonsense, hold up the picture, quarrel over every scene. On what grounds? That they're George Altman's girl, or Tiny Redder's girl, or Ed Doremus' or somebody else's girl and they think they can get away with it and they do for a while but it doesn't pay off. They don't hold up, they get a break and maybe make a hit but then they fizzle out. The public gets tired of them, they begin to lose their looks, they get fat, you can't even photograph them through a blue serge suit and no one can get a performance out of them because it was never there in the first place. But Jean's not one of those, either. She's a real professional. She'll be on time."

Gordon glanced at his watch. One minute to one.

"Where's that little son-of-a-bitch Devon?" Jean asked as she walked in and closed the door behind her.

"We were just talking about you, sugar," Henry said.

The silver curtains that backed the stage parted and a very small man stood there and looked at them through oversize tortoise-rimmed glasses.

"My angel," Jean said.

"Hello, Dev," Henry greeted him, "sorry about this but the suit's no good."

Devon moved slowly but lithely forward, letting the silver curtains half close behind him. He was almost bald and deeply sunburned. He wore a jacket of cream-colored tweed, tan trousers and a shirt and bow tie made of the same brown-and-white checked linen. He stood quietly regarding them with sad eyes behind his spectacles.

"My dear H.C.," the little man said in a deep and startlingly disproportionate voice, "we all make mistakes."

He said this in a way that left no doubt that in his mind the mistake was Henry's and he, Devon, was being charitable about it.

He looks like a spaniel, was Gordon's thought, *a small hairless spaniel*.

"Devon lover," Jean said, "this is my friend Gordon

Cram. Gordon, this is my genius Devon who makes every stitch I wear."

"She wears such becoming stitches," Gordon said. "How do you do, Mr. Devon."

"Nicely, thank you," said Devon, extending his little hand and giving Gordon such an aggressively masculine shake that Gordon winced with the pain. Devon's right shoulder went up as he performed this muscular greeting. "I feel as if I know you already, Mr. Cram. Your books, your books . . . when are you going to write another like *John Marriott*, that is what I want to know?"

"Gordon would like to know that himself," Henry answered. "Now, Devon, this suit works on Monday."

"I'm aware of that, H.C. But if you would tell me what you want, just give me a notion. A producer's idea of clothes is sometimes hard to grasp." The sneer was not concealed because it wasn't supposed to be concealed.

"Well, I can tell you what I *don't* want," Henry said, "and that's for Jean to look pregnant, which she does in that damned outfit."

"Put it on, Jean," Devon said, sighing, "and we'll see." He opened a door to the left of the stage and bellowed in his surprising baritone, "Miss Fielding's wine suit."

Jean wrapped a square of tulle around her hair, bit a Kleenex, and started to pull off her sweater.

"If you gentlemen would just step outside," Devon said, "thanks awfully."

The door closed firmly and Henry and Gordon were in the hall.

"Why does he get to stay?" Gordon asked.

Henry grinned.

They waited, feeling foolish.

"With that voice," Gordon said, "he'd do a hell of a job with *Asleep in the Deep*."

Devon opened the door again, "I may be wrong, but I think she looks heaven in it."

Jean was standing on the stage in front of a triple mirror wearing the disputed suit. She was running her hands from her waist to her thighs and back to her waist.

"What don't you like, love?" she asked Henry.

"That's what *I* want to know," Devon chimed in.

"Turn around, sugar," said Henry. "Look, Dev," he struck Jean across the bottom, "the skirt's too tight. Jean couldn't wear a skirt like this if she fasted till New Year's. Why not a circular skirt?"

"Because it's not the line this year, H.C.," Devon's voice rose with excitement, "my job is to anticipate the styles, to be ahead of fashion. This picture won't be released until fall. By then for God's sake you won't see a circular skirt *anywhere*."

"You'll see them on any woman who is built like Jean and has any sense."

"This jacket wouldn't do with a full skirt," Jean interposed, "it would be too long."

"That's the new line, too," Devon nearly cried, "longer jackets, emphasis on the bust and a pencil-slim skirt."

"Unfortunately," Henry said, "Miss Fielding doesn't have a pencil-slim behind."

"How sweet of you to remember," Jean said.

"I can see I'll have to make a new costume entirely.

144

That means keeping my people overtime. I don't know what Mr. A. will say."

"Let me worry about that," said Henry. "Make a new suit. And just in case you haven't read the script, then read it. Dress her for the character, not for the fashion magazines.'Style in a movie is ridiculous, anyhow. Charm and beauty is what we want. Jean has built her career with it. Otherwise she'd still be a Powers girl posing for street shots in *Harper's Bazaar*."

"As you wish," Devon held his hands to his forehead. He surrendered slightly, "Come to think of it, there's a little coat, tricky little thing, I made for 'The Crazy Countess' but they cut out the sequence. If you approve we could make a new skirt for that."

"Who did you make it for?" Henry asked.

"For what's-her-name, Sherry Laine."

"All right with you?" Henry turned to Jean.

"If it was made for that troll we don't have to worry about the bust emphasis," Jean said, "it'll be there, all built in."

Devon went to the rear door and called, "Laine's purple jacket from 'Crazy.' "

Jean began unbuttoning her blouse, "One second and I'll help you, precious," Devon said, looking pointedly at Henry and Gordon. They filed out, sighing heavily. Jean laughed and, turning around, drew open the blouse as Devon slammed the door.

"Jean ever work in burlesque?" Gordon asked.

"No," Henry laughed. "Devon is worse than a stage mother. Jean doesn't give a damn. She'd walk around naked if you'd let her."

"I'd let her," Gordon said. "I thought she seemed in a hurry to strip."

"That was for your benefit."

"Why mine? Oh yes, you're familiar with the territory."

"Don't be a cad," Henry said, "you sound like Sue."

"That wasn't on Sue's time, was it?"

"Long before," Henry said, "but you know women."

"Yep," Gordon said.

Again they waited, feeling foolish.

After Jean had tried on several suits and one was decided upon, Henry looked at his watch. "Nearly two and I have a conference. Good-bye, Jeanie, it's going to be all right."

"Good-bye, lover," she said, "you were sweet to do this. You too, Gordon."

"Enjoyed every minute. See you soon."

"I hope so," she said, looking right at him.

"Now don't you put us in a book, Mr. Cram," Devon implored, "don't you do that."

"I couldn't."

"I have my car," Henry said.

When they were driving back toward the New Building Henry said, "Did you notice that Jean let me take the rap for that suit? You'd never think to see her with Devon that she complains about everything he makes for her. That little bastard has every female star on the lot scared to death."

"Women are pitiful," Gordon said.

"And I had to miss my lunch and a *Time* interview," Henry grumbled. "I'm pitiful."

CHAPTER NINE *"S*UPPOSE I pick you up at seven-thirty?" Gordon had said to Alma on the telephone.

He was very nearly late. He cut himself shaving and hit his head coming out of the shower. The suit he wanted to wear wasn't pressed and the hotel valet had left for the day by the time he discovered it. Then he had some mysterious trouble starting the car. Even so it was not much past the half hour when he rang the doorbell.

There was a constricted feeling in his throat and he coughed nervously waiting for the door to be opened.

"Good evening, Mr. Cram."

"Good evening, Ivy."

"Mrs. Tavis is waiting."

Gordon was surprised to find her ready. She was sitting quietly by the fireplace, waiting.

"Hello," he said.

"Hello," she said.

Suddenly they had become strangers. It was as if she were someone he didn't know or hadn't seen for many years. Even the room seemed different. Had it only been last night?

"Will you have a drink?" she asked.

"If you will."

"I don't think so," she demurred, "I have a slight headache, but you have one."

"No, thanks, I had one before I came."

So this was the way it was going to be, he thought; she had made her decision and it was quite evident what it was.

"Won't you have another?" she asked with the new formality.

"I had too much last night."

"Oh," she looked surprised.

That got her, Gordon noticed, pleased, *and I'm not going to tell her that I was alone in that damned room. If she wants to find out let her ask.*

There was a pause while she took a cigarette from the silver box and Gordon lighted it for her.

"Shall we go along, then?" he asked.

"I'll get my things."

He watched her walking out of the room. His nervousness had gone now that he was here but instead there was an ache, an ache of loss.

She came back into the room.

"You look beautiful," he said.

She did; she also looked pale, but then she was always pale and she was especially quiet and composed, the way she had been in the beginning. She was wearing a plain black silk dress with no ornamentation other than its superlative cut and the outline of her figure beneath. Her slippers were gracefully wound ribbons of black satin.

"Those shoes," he said, regarding them admiringly, "could easily give a man a foot fetish."

"Aren't they pretty? I just got them. Ray sent them from Italy with Milly Rodgers."

Gordon didn't know why, but he was irritated by that. "If you're ready, let's go."

Alma picked up a pair of short snow-white gloves and her small black satin purse to which was pinned a diamond rose.

Gordon held out her broadtail coat, resisting the impulse to put his arms around her. She was so cool, so new and newly unapproachable.

"Where shall we go?" he asked when they were in his car.

"It doesn't matter," she said, "any place."

"Thursday night," he said, "so Romanoff's will be crowded. We'll run into people and not be able to talk." He thought for a minute. "Remember that little restaurant we found downtown the night we went to the movies?"

"That's a fine idea."

"Did you speak to Sue today?" he asked as they drove along.

"No, I didn't. I was supposed to lunch there but Sue left a message she had to take the children somewhere. Did you see Henry?"

"Worked with him all afternoon."

They made conversation all the way downtown as if

they had just met and were afraid both of silence and of discussing anything really personal.

The restaurant was a good choice. It was small, dimly lit and had a quiet, faintly clandestine atmosphere. There were very few other tables occupied and those mostly by couples intent on their food and each other.

"A drink first and then we'll think about dinner," Gordon said as they were seated. "Change your mind and have one, Alma."

"All right, a glass of champagne, nothing in it."

Gordon ordered a split of Pommery and a double Scotch old-fashioned for himself. He lit her cigarette and his own, thinking, *I wish she'd get it over with, come out and say it.*

He looked at her intently, studying every detail of her face, committing it to memory and then he noticed that there were mauve shadows under her eyes. "Did you sleep well?" he asked.

"I didn't sleep at all," she said. "When Ivy came in this morning I was in the kitchen making coffee. Ivy nearly dropped dead from the shock."

He laughed, "Well, I slept finally, but I was seized with a nightmare and that finished me. Christ, what a night. I was at the studio before nine this morning."

Their drinks arrived and they examined large menu cards and ordered dinner, though Gordon thought that he had never felt less like food.

"Hurray," Gordon lifted his glass, "by way of a toast."

Alma regarded him gravely over the edge of the champagne goblet. *As if she were seven years old,* he thought, *and drinking her milk, like a good little girl.*

150

Alma put her glass down but held onto it. *Here it comes,* he thought.

"I did what you told me to do," she said. "I've thought over everything you said."

Brace yourself, Gordon thought.

"Yes, Alma," he said.

"Perhaps you'd rather not talk about it now?"

"No, I'd rather," he said.

"Well," she said, "it's all right with me any way you want. I understand entirely that it will be just while you're here, but that's all right, you don't need to worry about me." She held her breath, looking at him and then she smiled for the first time that evening.

He waited for a long second, reviewing what she had said, what she meant. He was surprised and relieved and there was also another feeling, a new feeling.

He reached across the small table and held her cold hands and looked at her smiling at him, a proud, brave, unhappy smile.

He said carefully but unexpectedly, "I love you."

She stopped smiling. "Oh, thank God," she said.

"I've never said it, have I?" he asked in wonder at himself and her and at the warm strong emotion within him.

"No, you've never said it and I wanted to hear you say it to me, just once."

He knew now, perhaps he'd known for weeks, what he wanted to say but perhaps he hadn't admitted it because he'd been listening to his voice saying to Louise over and over, "I'll never leave you, Louise," perhaps he'd known last night and refused to accept it.

"Alma," he said, "it's going to be tough, there are

151

problems, things I haven't told you about. Alma, will you marry me?"

It wasn't until quite a while afterward that she would remember how quickly he had said it. Only afterward when she looked back to that instant of absolute joy, holding his hands across the table.

Some food came and was placed before them and she said, oblivious of the food and of the waiter, "I don't care how tough it will be, really, I don't care. I love you so much."

Out of habit rather than hunger Gordon picked up his knife and fork. He took a bite, chewed, swallowed and said, "Eat your dinner, darling."

She shook her head, speechless with delight.

He put down the knife and fork and said, "Let's get out of here."

"Oh, yes, please."

The waiter was concerned when Gordon asked for the check. The headwaiter appeared, looking worried.

"Is there anything wrong, sir?" he asked, looking at the uneaten rich food cooling on the plates.

"No, no, everything is fine," Gordon assured him, "we just remembered that we have another engagement. We should be there now, so if I could just have the check. . . ."

Gordon paid and they waited for his change, Alma looking as radiant in the dim room as if a light were shining on her. Neither of them later remembered their departure from the table.

When they were outside in the parking lot where they had left the car, Gordon took her in his arms, paying no attention to the passers-by and the traffic, and they held each other close with, for the first time, the passionless loving tenderness of two exhausted people who knew each other very well.

2

"I feel wonderful," Alma said, "do you?"

"Wonderful."

"Let's stay in bed for a week."

"Come closer." Gordon pulled the sheet over them. "It's an interesting idea," he said, "but I don't think I'd do much work on the script."

"Oh, the script," said Alma, "a secondary consideration."

"Not to Henry Calder. Where are the cigarettes?"

Alma gave him one. "Are you bothered about the script?"

"I think I am and I know Henry is," Gordon answered, "but lately I seem to have something else on my mind."

She rubbed her cheek against the side of his face. "Think about me every minute, every second, think about us."

He wound his arms around her.

She linked a leg through his and they remained that way for several minutes without speaking.

"Are there many problems?" she finally said.

"Some. But I don't want to discuss them now. I should be through by the first of the month. Then I'll go to New York and talk to Louise."

"The telephone?" she asked quietly.

"No, I couldn't do that."

"Of course not."

"It won't be easy for you," he said.

"And awful for her," she hoped that he would disagree.

"God, yes."

She had never heard that note in his voice before. She thought of Sue saying, "He was unnaturally kind to her."

"Oh, my love," she took his cigarette from him and rolled over, kissing his face, her fingernails biting into his shoulders, rubbing against him in a fit of love.

Reaching up over her head he turned off the light.

3

ALMA slept beside him in the big bed.

Gordon lay on his back listening to the absence of traffic noises, the suspension of sound that always kept him awake when he was out of the city. Alma stirred in her sleep, moving closer to him. He felt lonely awake when she was asleep, felt shut out and far from her, even though she was in the circle of his arm.

He tried to remember, and couldn't quite, the lines that he had always liked from "Ash Wednesday," something about the greater torment of love satisfied. This was love satisfied, lying here with Alma and it was torment but of a most acceptable sort, he thought, as he touched her shoulder and let his hand rest on the warm skin.

He turned over, groping in the dark for a cigarette.

I was so sure that I wouldn't leave Louise for anyone. But nothing could have stopped this, nothing.

He struck a match, shook it out. *I've been selfish and this is the peak of selfishness. I'm nearly forty and I've known a great many women and I've only loved two of them—two out of how many—but this is no night to count them. I'll go to New York and I'll tell Louise and perhaps she'll understand, not make it too difficult.*

Gordon lay awake staring into a darkness as blank and impenetrable as the years ahead. He couldn't put out of his mind the question of what would happen to Louise.

CHAPTER TEN

HREE thousand miles away as distance is measured and, by time, three hours ahead, Louise Cram was having one of her bad nights. Raising herself on one elbow she turned the face of the clock toward her. It was four o'clock, and she had to be up at eight.

Lying on the one flat pillow that she permitted herself, she wondered if she should get up and heat some milk; sometimes that helped. But she wasn't hungry and the thought of the bland, blotting-paper taste of warm milk was sickening. She could take a sleeping pill but she'd taken one the night before and the night before that and she was afraid to take them every night.

The apartment seemed full of mysterious night noises that fretted her nerves. Her back ached and her legs were tired from tensing at every sound. Considering this, she had a moment of actual loathing for her narrow bed and her narrow body. *Spinsterish*, she thought. When she and Gordon had first married they had often slept together

156

in this narrow bed, but had it ever really been comfortable? It hadn't mattered then . . .

She turned on her back and crossed her arms over her stomach. Her hands felt cold.

Cold. What a hateful word, cold is, she thought, *if I were dead I couldn't be more cold.* She drew the quilt over her. *I so often think about dying—perhaps I will die.* But that didn't seem likely for a woman who had so often and so desperately wished to die, to the extent of trying to kill herself, and who was still alive. It was probable that she would go on living for years and years, far beyond her allotted span, being bruised by time.

And Gordon, would he ever die and would she bury him and become a widow when she hadn't been a wife, really a wife, for so long?

But the thought of Gordon dying, dead, was hurtful to her. He was so alive, so avid for life and all that it had to offer. When he was here, in the apartment, even for the briefest time, the place vibrated with the power that he released; the click of the typewriter that indicated how his work was going, the shower running, his rummaging through the icebox, the bookshelves; even in the unhappy years of the close past, she found him exhilarating to have around, at least on those occasions when she hadn't actively wanted to throttle him, to maim him, to see him dead and weep for him.

For some reason she thought of him coming in from a walk, his face red and cold from the wind, kissing her cheek, gently, absently, from habit, as a child kisses his mother when he returns from school.

She thought of the little lines around his eyes that

deepened when he talked, of his hand holding a cigarette, of his shoulders; when they were first married she had slept with her head on his hard shoulder. In those days he didn't wear pajamas. She wondered if he did now.

What was the use of thinking of him in that way? "Better take a pill," she said, then rejected the idea.

She put on the light and with it the tiny, frightening noises were dispelled. The street outside was as quiet as a country lane, with only an occasional late taxi and the sound of muffled, late laughter to disturb it.

Louise looked over at the other empty bed that matched hers and wondered why she kept it in her room. A symbol, she supposed, a suitable device for a crest: empty bed rampant.

Gordon hadn't slept in that bed for years, she knew exactly how many. When he was at home he slept in the smaller room on the other side of the bathroom but all the same she liked knowing that he was there, and when she was awake she could hear the mild protest of bed springs as he turned over in sleep.

How would she feel having a man in her room again, in her bed: after all this time alone to listen to heavier, alien breathing, to feel another warmer body beside her. It had been a long time.

If she had a lover Gordon wouldn't care, she couldn't even delude herself that it would matter to him. If he had any feeling about it, would it not be one of relief?

The sense of the past was stifling, suddenly oppressive, a closing-in of memory so that she was returned in her mind to the time when Gordon had been her lover, her first lover. Did he ever think of those days, did he ever remember her running up the three flights of stairs to that room he had lived in, the room with the lumpy bed and the surprising bright blue rug on the floor?

"Gordon," she had said, out of breath, "I . . . if this is what you want . . . I mean, if it's me, well I'm glad."

He'd laughed—how could he help it—what a preposterous speech!

"Sit down and catch your breath," he had said, still laughing, "and take your hat off."

And then he had been kind to her, infinitely kind and loving and understanding, so that holding him she had whispered in his ear, "Oh, Gordon, you were right, it would have been foolish to wait."

That had been the first time and from then on he had been her lover for over a year, the happiest year of her life. She had been a reader at Dover House then, making very little money and giving ten precious dollars of it to her mother. Gordon had no money; with the small advance that Dover House had given him on the novel that was to be his first published novel he had rented a room and a typewriter. But it had been a good time— she had not realized then quite how good—there was so much ahead to be done and Gordon was so eager to do it, to finish his book, to go around the world on a freighter, to go around the world on a lush, elegant French boat. All she had wanted was for him to finish the book and for herself to get a better job at Dover House and above everything else she wanted to marry Gordon Cram.

Every once in a while on a Saturday night she would tell her mother that she was spending the night with her friend Irene. As soon as she finished at Dover House she'd go to Gordon's room. She'd send him out to buy what they would need for breakfast (by saving on car-fare and cigarettes all week they had enough for a good breakfast on Sunday). When he had gone she'd clean and air the room thoroughly and make the bed with fresh sheets. By that time Gordon would be back carrying the brown paper bags of cornflakes and eggs and bacon and milk. Then they would get into the newly made bed, holding the other close, close.

Later they would dress and go out to have a late dinner at a Chinese restaurant which was two blocks away, or sometimes just a hot dog at the Nedick's stand on the corner, and many cups of coffee. Somehow they managed to drink innumerable cups of coffee together. After dinner they'd take long walks. Sometimes on Fifth Avenue to look in the shop windows and in the spring and summer along Riverside Drive. They'd look at the battleships anchored in the wide waters of the Hudson River and watch the sailors with their arms around their girls. Across the river the yellow lights of Pali-sades Park glittered and were as fantastic as a child's idea of Oz and the big Linit sign on the Jersey side, a moving ribbon of light, paused once every minute to spell "The time is now . . ." In the hot summer night that sign gave them both a sharp sense of the passage of time and of themselves alone in the great city watch-ing the minutes being written on the night, reflected in the dark river while they sat on a park bench eating an Eskimo Pie.

Every Sunday afternoon they met whether or not she had been able to stay the night before and Louise would sit at the rented typewriter and copy on long sheets of white paper (which her sister, who worked in a law office, brought home for her) what Gordon had written during the week. Not only did she copy it but they went over every line, discussing, even arguing over each sentence. They were in love with the novel those nights as much as they were in love with each other.

Did I know how lucky I was? Louise often asked herself. During those days, before we were married, Gordon was mine, he was in love with me, he needed me, I was essential; there might have been other girls then, but not often. He was busy and he was poor, he was single-minded in that time; the book came first and I was part of the book. He needed me to finish the book, I was a sounding board and he needed me for comfort and encouragement. He needed me to make love to on that awful bed in that awful room.

Though she was then sure (surer than ever since) of Gordon's love for her, she had never for a second been sure that he wanted to marry her even if he had had enough money.

But she was determined to marry him. She had to have him. This other way there was no security for her. Louise would shake, literally shake, at the thought of losing him. *We must get married*, she'd think, lying on the davenport in her mother's living room in Jackson Heights. In spite of having read everything she could get hold of since the age of twelve and living with a family tormented by turbulent relationships, Louise had faith in the power of the wedding band to bind a man, so much faith that she would repeat again and again her private litany, *We must get married as soon as we can.*

And what's left of this happy time? So little, so little

for me except that I remember it gratefully. It isn't connected with rage or bitterness or terrible scenes like what followed. If that first memory were gone then I would kill myself and I'd make sure this time that I didn't fail.

Now there is only his work left. "To Louise" had been the dedication of the first book, then "To My Wife," the second. When the third was being written we'd been married for two years and he had a secretary, so I no longer did the typing for him and that book (the one about the war in Spain) had said "For L.B.C." Those three novels remain, those we shared and to some extent we still share at least the books. It's good to be important to a man's work but it's not enough for a woman. It's not enough for me.

She got out of bed quickly and went to her closet. At the back she had hung his old bathrobe and, reaching in for it, she took it out and shivering a little she put it on. It was an old dark blue-and-gray-striped flannel bathrobe that Gordon hadn't used in years. She'd saved it from a stack of clothes he'd asked her to give away. She drew it around her now, glad of its warmth. There was something reassuring about it; she put her hands in the darned pockets, rubbed her cheek against the worn shoulder.

"Now that I'm up, I'll smoke a cigarette," she spoke aloud. Like many people who have been much alone she talked to herself. "If I don't feel sleepier after the cigarette I'll give in and take the pill."

There was something alarming to her in this new reliance on sleeping pills; all those stories in the papers of people taking an overdose accidentally, or not at all accidentally, deliberately taking them out of the box, counting them, swallowing them. . . .

Understanding the temptation was why it frightened her. Mary Fraser, who worked at Dover House as the editor of juvenile books, took one every night of her life and expressed concern only when she heard the rumor that they were bad for one's sex life.

Louise was afraid of them especially on nights like this, when life stretched ahead a flat, drab plain. She could understand wanting to sleep and not awaken, to give up in sleep the defeating struggle of holding on to someone who didn't want to be held.

Of course, Gordon had said time and time again that he would never leave her. Sometimes she played with the idea of leaving him. How astonished he would be! Perhaps then he would ask her to come back to him, tell her that everything had changed and that he knew that he needed her, needed her and wanted her.

But she might as well be honest with herself—that much discipline she must insist upon—so that she could say to herself, I faced the truth of it. Gordon would never need her or want her again. He was safe and secure and sure. All that was once between them had gone. . . . Or was she wrong, was there a place in his memory where the love waited unchanged, until the day he would remember and, remembering, love her again?

She looked at her room. It was not a particularly feminine room, although as she had it to herself she could have indulged any fancies. But she had never been interested in furniture and decoration any more than she was interested in clothes. People admired the apartment; it was comfortable and attractive but she knew that it had no elements that made it either original or individual. This bedroom, except for the bookshelves, might be the bedroom of any married couple. It was the sort of room, undistinguished and agreeable, that one saw photographed for the less glossy "home" magazines. It contained the beds, a dresser, a highboy and a vanity of the same wood and period, excellent reproductions which she had bought at a department store when they married. The strange thing about the room, she thought, was that although it was not especially feminine it was a room so evidently without a man. Louise smiled, remembering what Mary Fraser had said at lunch the other day, "The most important article in a woman's bedroom is a man."

She went to the ladder-back chair, the one upon which Gordon always used to hang his jacket.

I suppose I should never have made him marry me but I've been punished for it and so has Gordon. We've been punished unfairly, more than we deserved, but who can say—who controls the meting out of punishment?— was there an order to it or was it all the crazy chance that occasionally and coincidentally gives a semblance of trial and error, justice and recompense, to the pattern of people's lives?

She had once believed that it was all figured out down to the final infinitesimal tick of time but now she doubted that as she had come to doubt everything. Doubt, the most corroding poison in the human mind. Had she once been so simple as to believe that it would ever work out happily?

Looking at the hands of the clock she again thought about Gordon. What was he doing? It was one o'clock

164

in California and he was probably sound asleep. She longed to hear his voice. Of course she could call him, but it would sound silly. "I can't sleep so I thought I'd telephone." When would he come back? He hadn't mentioned anything in his letters except that the script was going more slowly than he had expected. And when he returned it would make little difference. He would give her an expurgated account of his trip, then talk about the job he had finished and the job he would do next. Nothing personal, that was over and done, and one of the worst features of a wakeful night like this was that she ever let herself forget that it was over and done.

The doctor had said, "Other marriages survive this sort of thing." But she had learned that no marriage is "Other marriages."

Suddenly she began to cry.

She fumbled her way into the bathroom, "I can't stand another minute," she whispered resolutely. She opened the medicine cabinet and took out the small paper box with two kinds of capsules, red and yellow, and the instructions on the cover: *One or two if necessary for sleep Mrs. G. Cram.* She looked at the pills, trying to count, at quick glance. Surely there were over two dozen, and sixteen was enough.

She turned on the cold-water tap and let it run for a moment. Then she filled a glass and took it and the box back into the bedroom. Sixteen would probably work fast. She'd take them in bed. Methodically she turned off the bathroom light behind her.

She shook out a handful of capsules.

Then slowly she put them back one by one on the white cotton wool, every one but a yellow capsule. As

165

the doctor's nurse had suggested, she bit an end of it so that it would work more rapidly and swallowed it.

She took off Gordon's robe and hung it back in the closet on the last hook. Then she turned down the bedspread and got into the other bed that used to be his and put out the light. After all, he would be coming back from California one of these days and this might be *the* time. She would be a fool to kill herself. She folded her hands and lay on her back like an effigy, composed, waiting for the drug to take effect. It was nearly five o'clock, three hours earlier in California, she thought drowsily. She rolled over. "Good night, darling," she murmured to the pillow.

She fell into a sleep so deep that the telephone rang and rang for a long time before it penetrated the thick, drugged sleep. Rang and rang and rang, before she shook herself half awake and got up stumbling and dizzy to answer, ringing and ringing and ringing, shrill and loud through the early empty quiet. She thought it would never stop that infernal ringing and ringing.

2

WHEN Alma awakened Gordon wasn't there. She looked at the crystal clock on the bedtable. It was ten minutes past two. She drew the covers about her shoulders, wondering what she had done with her nightgown. There was a line of light under the bathroom door.

"Gordon," she called, "darling?"

He came out of the bathroom wearing his shorts and socks and holding a shoe.

166

"I'm out one shoe," he said. "Why are you awake? I thought I was being quiet."

"I just woke up," Alma said, "I hate to wake up and not find you."

"I couldn't get to sleep so I thought I'd go to the hotel."

"Are you worried, darling?"

"No, I know this is good for us," he said, kneeling to look under the bed for his shoe.

"I do too. I do too."

"Are you hungry, Alma?"

"Shall I make us some eggs?"

"I don't want eggs," he said, "I'll see what I can find in the kitchen."

Alma lay back on her pillows, yawned and stretched, sighed with content. She thought, still bemused with love and sleep, that this was the happiest moment of her life. She couldn't imagine possibly being happier except of course when it was all settled and they were married but then it would be different.

And how wonderful that this was happening to her! Not only had she fallen in love but Gordon loved her and they need never be apart. Her fears of the loneliness ahead had vanished. She would have a real marriage, not like the travesty with Ray to whom she had never felt married. She would make this work, and she'd make up to Gordon as much as she could for anything that had gone wrong in his life with Louise. How lovely to think that she need never be alone again!

Gordon came back from the kitchen with two glasses of milk and a plate with two tall, ragged slices of chocolate cake.

"Ivy is a great woman with the cake," he said. "See that we always have chocolate layer cake when we're married. Don't just lure me with it and then forget like the ladies in the ads whose husbands are always leaving the house looking pained."

"Those ladies don't neglect the larder. It's far, far worse than that," Alma said.

"Ah, I see, poor husbands," he said. "By the way, will Ivy mind if we get married?"

"She'll be greatly relieved, I think," Alma said. "Where will we live?"

"New York," he said. "Where else would we live?"

"Will we ever come out here?"

"We'll come out here once a year," he said. "Maybe in the summer so we can take a house at the beach. But I want to take you to Europe first. I want to take you to Venice on our honeymoon, to the Lido, it's that kind of a place. Wait till you see it!"

"It's good just to talk about it."

"I've never been a good husband," he went on, "never wanted to, I guess."

Alma waited, her mouth full of cake.

"But I will be," he said.

Alma swallowed.

"I used to want to know all about women, but I see now that if it's the right woman then it's all women. Do I make myself clear?"

"Not very, but I don't care if I am the one."

"You are."

"Then come back to bed," she said.

"Give me the glass and the plate."

He put them on the table in the hall, then returned

to the bed and stood looking down at her. With his finger
he traced slowly and unbelievingly the curve of her
cheek and her chin and her throat, down to her bare,
smooth stomach.

"Where do you suppose your shoe got to?" she asked.

"To hell with the shoe," he said.

CHAPTER ELEVEN C AREFULLY, so as not to disturb Alma, Gordon drew himself out of bed; the sheets whispered and the bed springs creaked treacherously but she did not stir. Quietly he made his way to the bathroom and began to dress.

He looked at himself in one of Alma's many mirrors, surprised that his face wasn't pale with sleeplessness. This kind of insomnia must be neurotic, he thought. He had worked hard all day and the evening had been full, to say the least, yet he hadn't slept for more than an hour.

Having dressed, he returned to the bed and kissed the top of Alma's head. She turned over, murmuring his name, to the side of the bed that he had been lying on.

He had left his car discreetly in the garage. He got into it and drove toward the hotel, then changed his mind. It was six-thirty and room service at the Bel Vista didn't start until seven-thirty. There was a drive-in at the corner of Linden and Wilshire that stayed open all night.

It was evident that the day was going to be clear and sunny. The sky was milky blue, nearly white, as if it were still too soon for the blue pigment to manifest itself; the sunlight was thin and cool and colorless. It reminded Gordon of the light, pure and shining, around the holy figure in all Italian primitives.

As he turned down Linden he passed the big white house at the corner where Jean Fielding lived. Her chrome yellow car was in the driveway and he saw her come out of the house and walk quickly to it. She looked young and thin and, he thought, attractive in slacks, a bandana tied around her head. Six-thirty and on her way to the studio. No welders worked harder than these glamour girls. She looked lonely and resolute. It would be twelve hours before the stages at R.A.M. would go dark and Jean could turn her famous and fatigued figure toward home again.

As he went along Gordon recalled her saying at the Calders' that she expected to finish her picture next week. He wondered if he had only imagined there was an invitation in the way she had said that to him. In the cool sane daylight, he thought it strange that they had never got around to each other. He had known her for years and often had the idea that she thought it might be fine.

"Too late now," he said, grinning in the windshield mirror.

He parked at the drive-in and gave a sleepy girl his order for orange juice, toast, coffee and two fried eggs,

171

sunny side up. The fresh morning and the glimpse of Jean had been stimulating. He was hungry.

Twenty minutes later he was back at the hotel. It still had a shuttered, night look to it, though by now the sun was entirely up. No one was in sight but an old man sweeping the veranda and a Filipino boy dragging a garden hose over the lawn. It was then that he discovered to his annoyance that he had forgotten his room key and would have to go around to the desk in the lobby.

"119, please."

"Oh, yes, Mr. Cram." The night clerk was still on duty. Gordon thought that he looked at him strangely. He wished that he had left a razor at Alma's.

The clerk turned to the trellis of little boxes behind him and from one he took a key and a batch of the white-paper slips on which messages were written.

"These all for me?" Gordon asked, surprised.

He glanced at the top message: CALL NEW YORK OPERATOR 328, Gordon read, and beneath it written in red pencil was the one word URGENT. All the others were the same. Nine of them.

Gordon walked down the hallway to his room, past the closed, quiet doors each with a Do Not Disturb sign hung on the door knob. It must be Hammond trying to reach him, he was thinking, his agent. He looked at his watch. Nearly seven. That meant nearly ten in New York.

He stopped outside his door and picked up the morning papers and a duplicate stack of messages, each with the red-penciled URGENT.

"Hammond probably wants to know what I'm going to do about *Holiday's* offer." He unlocked the door.

172

The room was dark, the draperies still drawn at the windows as they had been left by the maid the night before.

Gordon stood at the door and looked in as if he half expected to find someone there. Then, deliberately slow in his movements, he closed the door, opened the windows, went into the bathroom, brushed his teeth and turned on the electric wall heater so that the room would be warmed when he took his shower.

He read the messages again, every twenty minutes from 4:25 to half an hour ago . . . . Even though Hammond was notorious for his devotion to the telephone, why should he have called so early, at an hour that would have awakened Gordon? And why would he leave a message marked URGENT?

He opened a new package of cigarettes and lit one. If it was not Hammond, then it must be some girl in New York, not Louise. She was that rare thing, a woman with an aversion to the telephone, especially to long-distance conversations, and anyhow they had nothing to say to each other that could not be put in a letter. The need to hear another's voice was for those in love. Of course, it could be *about* Louise. She might have been hurt, run over in the street, or suddenly taken ill. Or perhaps she had tried to kill herself again.

He reached for the telephone.

"Long distance, please," he said to the hotel operator.

It was several minutes before they answered and Gordon, listening to the insistent, unanswered ringing, felt an obscure anger at the whole thing.

"Long Distance."

173

"Operator 328 in New York," Gordon said, looking again at the messages to check the number.

"And what is your name and number?"

"Gordon Cram, Room 119 at the Bel Vista Hotel."

There was a clicking and then with incredible swiftness he heard a voice say, "New York."

There was a longer wait until Operator 328 came on, then the Beverly Hills operator said, "Crestview 1-1900, Mr. Cram, W.H. on the line."

Operator 328 repeated his name asking, "Is that C as in Candy or B as in Boy r-a-m?"

"C as in Candy," said Beverly Hills.

"Crestview 1-1900," the New York Operator said, pausing after the first numeral in the New York manner.

Gordon wondered what W.H. stood for. He put out a cigarette and lit another. His hand faltered as he struck the match.

"What the hell is the matter with me?" he thought irritably.

The Beverly Hills operator said, after a silence, "We'll call you, Mr. Cram, New York is tracing your call."

"It isn't *my* call, they're calling me," Gordon said, "and it's urgent."

"Yes sir, we'll call you," the operator said. She sounded bored.

"I'll hold on," Gordon said.

"Beverly Hills?"

"Yes, operator?"

"Does your party know what number is trying to reach him?"

"No, I don't," Gordon said. "What does W.H. mean, girls?"

They didn't answer and he listened while they talked to each other in their rapid codes and by the names of their cities. There were clickings and ringings and buzzings; it all seemed to take an inordinately long time and, straining to hear, he thought that one of the more remote voices asked for Regent 4-6230, which was his telephone number, but perhaps he imagined it. His hands holding the telephone grew damp with sweat and he again put out and again lit a cigarette.

Now he heard a steady, ordinary ringing which then stopped as someone picked up the receiver.

The New York operator said, "We are ready with your call to Beverly Hills."

The Beverly Hills operator said, "Go ahead, Mr. Cram."

"Gordon?" a woman's voice said. "Is it you, Gordon?"

"Yes," he said. He didn't quite recognize the voice. "Louise?"

"Oh, Gordon," she said, and he knew that she'd either been crying or had a terrible cold.

"What's the matter?"

"Something has happened," she said, "I've been trying to get you for hours."

"I can't hear you very well," he said, "are you all right?"

"I'm all right. I mean it's not me. Gordon, listen, can you hear me now?"

"I can hear you now," he said.

"It seems so awful to have to tell you this way, over the phone. I don't know how to tell you; he's dead, Gordon, he died, early this morning."

"Who?" Gordon shouted. "Who died?"

"The baby," she said. "Our baby."

Gordon didn't say a word.

"Are you still there? Didn't you hear me?"

"I'm here," he said. "I'm here, darling."

"I feel so awful about it, so sad, now there's nothing, nothing."

"Take it easy, Loulie," he said, "tell me what happened. Try to stop crying."

"They don't know, really. I was there last Sunday. He seemed fine, so much better than last time. I could hardly believe it . . . such a change in less than a month. And he'd grown, too," she paused, he heard her blowing her nose, then she continued, "I brought him some things they said he'd like, some wooden beads and colored paper. He did like them, Gordon, he loved them. He seemed to know me this time, he really did. He even looked unhappy when I had to leave," her voice stopped abruptly.

"Go on, Louise," Gordon said.

"I had a talk with the doctor that day and he was pleased with his progress. They said that if he continued to improve I could have him with me this summer while you were away . . ."

"Don't cry, dear, tell me what happened."

"Gordon, he was trying to get away. Even Dr. Springer admits that. I can't bear it."

"I don't understand, Lou, how could he get away?"

"Springer says that they noticed he'd been restless all day. They had a little trouble with him at lunch. They put him to bed early, in a little room by himself so that he wouldn't disturb the others. He must have awakened in the night and got out in some way. He went as far as the big wall and climbed up. Then he must have been frightened and lost his balance and fallen because they found him there about six o'clock this morning with his neck broken. Dr. Springer says there wasn't any pain; at least that, no pain."

"Loulie, Loulie, Loulie," Gordon said.

"And he had the beads with him, in his poor little hand. They'd taught him to string them. Oh, my God!"

Gordon felt a sudden sharp pain. He realized that his cigarette had burned down to his finger and he hadn't noticed it. He said, "Look, I'll get on a plane today. The first one that I can get on. I'll call you and tell you after I get the reservation. I think there's one that can get me in tonight."

"I'm glad," she said. "Thank you, Gordon."

He felt ashamed and through the shock he now felt the beginning of sadness. "Take it easy," he said, "can someone stay with you?"

"I'll be all right if you're coming," she said. "What shall I do about the arrangements, they want to know?"

"Tell them," Gordon said slowly, "that all the arrangements will be made when I arrive."

He heard her sob, then she asked, "Can you get away, what about the picture?"

"I'll be there," he said, "I want to be with you."

She began to cry again. "Gordon, you are being very good to me."

"I'll call you as soon as I get the reservation. Ask the doctor to give you a shot of something and go to bed. Will you, Loulie?"

"I will," she said, "but it's so sad."

"Yes," he said, "it is."

For a while after he had finished talking to Louise he remained sitting on the edge of the bed staring at the wall. "Poor little thing," he thought, the sadness becoming a special sadness for the child whom he hadn't seen for almost a year, not since he had driven up there with Louise. Those visits upset them both but Louise went faithfully every third Sunday, and she had been better able to accept it than Gordon. That gray stone house set far from the road, the high stone walls encircling it (how could the poor little fellow have scaled that wall?), the well tended lawns that no one ever walked on, the gloomy faces of the nurses and the synthetic optimism of Dr. Springer, who was in charge of the establishment.

Louise had sounded devastated, probably from the shock. What an unfortunate way for it to have happened, a pitiable way. Poor Louise, she'd been so grateful for what little comfort he had given her. Thinking of that now only added to his feeling of irrational, unexpected grief.

Alma. He straightened up and shook himself. His thoughts went to Alma and her face when he had asked her to marry him. How odd to think that the death of a child who had hardly lived and whose existence she did not suspect might affect her life.

He tried to think of what he must do. His packing wouldn't take long. He had to tell Henry Calder, so that Henry could get someone else on the script at once. He'd understand; anyway, this had been an unlucky script. There had been trouble with it from the beginning.

But first he'd have to tell Alma. As soon as he'd arranged about the plane, he'd go back to her house. She was probably still sleeping, just as he had left her.

CHAPTER TWELVE $\mathscr{A}$LMA lay for a long
while in the wide tumbled bed, not ready to relinquish
the night, thinking of Gordon with a newly safe love
which made her burrow her head into the soft pillow
on which his head had lain.

Then she pressed the button of the cloisonné bell to
summon Ivy, rose and went into the bathroom. She
looked for evidence of Gordon's having been here, but
there were none. The pale green towel which he had
used was folded neatly, monogram in the center, the
tablet of soap was rinsed and put back in its own china
dish on the washstand. Without knowing just why she
laughed as she took the top off the toothpaste. Never had
she known this feeling of unconditional delight.

By the time she came out wearing a fresh nightgown
and bedjacket, Ivy had smoothed and straightened the
bed, the eiderdown was folded at the foot, the pillows
reassembled and piled at Alma's place and Ivy herself
waited with the breakfast tray.

"Good morning, Mrs. Tavis, sun's out for a change."

"Warm enough for a sun bath?" Alma asked, climbing into bed.

Ivy said that she thought it was. She placed the tray over Alma's knees and gave her the morning papers and the Hollywood *Reporter*.

Ivy opened the windows wide. Sunlight poured into the room, prodigal, honey gold, reflecting itself in the mirrors, polishing everything it touched, making prisms and rainbows in the glass objects in the room.

While Alma drank her first cup of coffee Ivy stepped through the long windows that opened onto the patio and began to dust a cot that Alma used for sun bathing.

Alma enjoyed her breakfast. Everything tasted delicious; the English muffin toasted, buttered and quartered, the strawberry jam, the cold grapefruit cut into neat little sections, the strong coffee.

Gordon would probably be at the studio by now. She wanted so much to hear his voice that she put her hand on the telephone. But he'd be busy. If she hadn't heard from him by lunch time, she'd call him. He'd be working hard this morning.

Her hand stayed on the telephone. He would be working hard to finish the script so that he could leave for New York to tell his wife. Then, suddenly thinking of his going away, she nearly cried out. Of course it wouldn't be for long and she'd make him promise to call her every night and when it was over it would be the last time they'd be parted.

"Anyway, he said it will be at least three weeks before he can finish the script," she thought comfortably, pouring another cup of coffee.

She decided that she would call Sue. Gordon hadn't said that she could not tell Sue. She'd swear her to secrecy, make her promise on the heads of her children not to tell anyone, not even Henry. She simply had to tell her. She might never have met Gordon if it hadn't been for Sue. Besides, Sue would be a bit annoyed about their having left so early the other night. Alma put down her cup so determinedly that it jiggled everything on the tray and dialed Sue's number. The truth was, she acknowledged, that she couldn't keep it to herself a second longer.

Sue answered the telephone with her usual expectant "Hello."

"Good morning, Susie."

"Ah," said Sue, "The Lady of Shallot. Aren't you up early?"

"You're cross with me."

"Furious," Sue said, "you're a great help to the anxious hostess."

"I've got something to tell you that you won't believe."

"What?"

"Can't you guess?"

"Tell me, for the love of God."

"Gordon has asked me to marry him."

"I'm speechless," Sue said. "Are you going to?"

"The sooner the better."

"Come on right over, we have to talk about this."

"Promise not to tell anyone, not even Henry. Promise me."

"I promise, but hurry up. We can't talk on the phone."

"I'm just finishing breakfast and I want a little of this sun, then I'll be with you."

"Alma," Sue asked in a different tone, "you're not, I must ask you, because, well—Alma, you're not . . . ?"

"Don't be quaint!" Alma said, laughing.

Then they both began to laugh crazily with pleasure and relief.

"Isn't it wonderful," Alma kept on saying.

"I can't get over it," Sue would answer and soon, both saying that it was impossible to discuss it over the telephone, they were talking and laughing and planning in the special shorthand talk of close friends, in confusion and delight.

2

GORDON stood in front of Alma's door, squinting in the sun, which now was high and hot overhead. The cloudless sky seemed close and smooth; up and down the street the parked cars had their tops down and sprinklers were splashing on the lawns, the days of rain forgotten.

Gordon rang the bell.

Only a few hours ago he had walked out of this house and driven away, resolved to do something about his life, something that would have been drastic and unalterable. Now as he pressed the doorbell, he was aware that temporarily at least that was not possible. This morning he had had the illusion of having a free choice, now before noon had come there was clearly no choice whatever.

No one came to the door and he rang again. Where

was Ivy? It wasn't likely that Alma would be out this early. It was ludicrous that at this moment he had to stand on the doorstep feeling rather like a man selling brushes.

He put his ear against the lintel and heard within the whirring, whining sound of a vacuum cleaner.

He rapped against the door with his fist. The noise of the machine stopped and the door suddenly opened.

"Oh, Mr. Cram," Ivy said, "good morning."

"Mrs. Tavis awake yet?"

"Yes sir, come right in. She's taking a sun bath, sorry I didn't hear the bell."

"Would you tell Mrs. Tavis that I'd like to see her right away?"

"Yes sir. Won't you wait in here?"

He followed her into the living room. It was the first time, he thought, that he'd ever seen it by daylight.

Ivy arranged the curtains at the window. "Too bright in here?"

"Fine, just fine," he said absently.

"I'll go tell her," Ivy said, leaving the room.

He sat down on one of the low white-brocade chairs by the fireplace. There were cigarettes and matches beside him on a table and a white camellia floating in a crystal dish. It was all so like Alma, he thought, so arranged, so spotless, so delicate and impractical, not a house for a man.

Sitting in the chair, he thought of the first night that he had ever been in this room, when he had brought her home from the Calders'. He had sat in this chair smoking a cigarette and he had overturned the ash tray.

"It really doesn't matter," Alma had said earnestly, "please don't bother about it."

"I'm quite a clumsy man," he'd said, "here, let me." With his handkerchief he brushed the ashes from the white chair and the carpet.

He remembered kneeling there looking up at her.

"Let me fix a drink," she'd said.

She seemed rather nervous when she brought it to him. He was standing, elbow on the mantel, surveying the fragile room.

"Do sit down," she'd said.

He'd taken the glass from her and put it with some care on a comparatively sturdy table. Then without a word and not touching her, he kissed her.

He put his arms around her and held her, feeling against his body the yielding compliance of hers. He kissed her again and this time she kissed him back.

"Oh . . ." she'd said. Then, still standing, clinging and pressing against each other wordlessly in the bright room, they suddenly let go and both had laughed and sat down together on the sofa.

"I suppose," he'd said, "that you knew I've wanted to do that all night."

"And I wanted you to."

He leaned forward and put his mouth against the skin where her dress was cut away between the breasts, "That was something else I wanted to do."

He raised his head and she inclined hers and they slowly kissed again.

He looked at her, the question unspoken.

She had stood up and he followed her down the hall

184

to her bedroom. They had left the lights burning bright and wasted in the living room all through the night.

"God damn it," he swore now.

Ivy came to the door, "Will you come right in, Mr. Cram, and Mrs. Tavis says will you have a cup of coffee?"

"Yes," he said, "if it isn't a lot of trouble."

The bedroom door was open but Alma wasn't there.

"Hello, darling," she called, "out here."

She was lying on her back in the sun, her pale skin glistening with oil.

"How wonderful you're here," she greeted him. "Will you have some coffee?"

"Yes, I've told Ivy," he said.

There was something inappropriate about standing here, the sun making him feel hot and heavy in his woolen suit and Alma stretched out naked before him. "Could we go inside, Alma?"

She got up. "I want to hug you but I'd ruin your suit."

She began patting herself with a towel to remove the oil. There was something loving and sensual in the way she did it; he thought she would have been brisker about it if she'd been alone.

Tell her now, right now, something within him spoke. *How can I tell her while she's stark naked?*

He picked up her robe, a tailored one of thin white silk, and draped it over her back.

His hands rested for a moment on her shoulders. They felt small and young. She took his hands and put them over her breasts, arching back so that her cheek touched his.

"It's sweltering," he said, "let's go in."

185

"Yes, let's go in."

"No, Alma, listen," he said, "I must talk to you."

She pulled the belt tight around her waist. "Anything wrong, darling?"

They stepped through the window to the cool bedroom.

"I was lying there in the sun," Alma said, going to him, "wondering when you'd call and then you appear. It's magical."

He started to speak but there was a tap at the door. "Come in, Ivy."

Ivy carried in a small table and set it before Alma.

"I don't want to be disturbed or take any telephone calls while Mr. Cram is here," Alma said.

Ivy went out and closed the door behind her. Gordon knew that he must speak now and quickly.

He stared at the pocket of her robe which had her name embroidered on it in lower-case letters . . . alma.

"Two sugars and a dot of cream," she said, giving him the cup of coffee.

"I'm leaving for New York," he said abruptly, "at two o'clock."

"But you're not finished with the picture."

"Something has come up." He made himself look at her levelly. "We said a lot of things last night."

"Nothing has changed, has it, didn't you mean what you said, or have I done something?"

He couldn't stand that, or the look on her face, or the sudden utter droop of her body. He came over to her and put an arm around her gently, "You haven't done a thing, baby, you never could."

He felt her relax within the circle of his cautious arm.

"You frightened me."

"Your coffee will get cold," he said. "Drink it."

Obediently she lifted her cup but it trembled in her hands. She set it down and looked with astonishment at her shaking wrist.

Gordon picked up the cup and held it to her lips as she drank a few sips (he had done that once before, in the hospital with Louise, but then it had been tea).

"That's enough, thank you," she said politely. She folded her hands in her lap to control the trembling. "Now tell me."

In the instant that he searched for words he thought that this would be the first time that he had ever told anyone. Louise's family knew, the Calders knew, but not from him. Yet now he was going to tell someone, who after all, was a part of it.

As he talked he noticed that Alma looked puzzled at first, then surprised. It was not easy. As the facts of the child's birth came from him he listened to himself as though a stranger were speaking.

Finally, as he neared the finish and the full secret was out, all except the news of the child's death, he saw the color gradually, then totally leave her face.

At last she spoke. "And no one knows?"

"Only a few. We said the child had been stillborn."

"Poor little thing," Alma said, "if only it had been."

"Nothing has been right between Louise and me since then. It's unreasonable, perhaps, but that's the way it's been all these years; it hasn't been easy for her."

"But will she stand in the way of a divorce? I mean

187

it can't hurt the child the way it would a child that lived with you, a normal child, and if you are in love with someone else. . . ."

"I'm in love with you," he said, "but I can't ask her for a divorce."

Alma's eyes went blank. "It doesn't matter to me, really darling, just as long as we can be together and I know that you love me. It doesn't matter."

"Baby, we can't be together, not for a while, anyway."

"Would it upset her so much if she heard about me, you mean?" Alma asked.

"I haven't told you everything yet," he said. "I was going to ask her for a divorce and make arrangements to take care of the child, an annuity or something. Then Louise called this morning to tell me that the child died yesterday."

Alma was first unable to speak, tears came into her eyes and she shook her head from side to side.

"Oh, my God!" said Alma.

She drew one single shuddering breath. "Poor Gordon," she said, "poor darling."

Gordon dampened a towel with cold water and held it against her forehead and the nape of her neck.

"I'm so sorry," she said, "I'm so awfully sorry for you."

"It's a tough break," he said.

"I was too happy." She mused, "Last night and this morning, I was much too happy."

"I'm leaving for New York at two this afternoon," he said, "I'll keep in touch, but I don't know when I'll be back. I'm sorry you had to get in the middle of this."

188

"But if the child is dead," Alma said, "doesn't that mean that you're free?"

"I don't think so," he said. "I haven't thought it out at all. Can you understand that?"

"You won't be back," she said.

"Sure I will," he said, "I'll be back in the fall."

"This is April," she said. She lifted her shoulders and let them drop. "You'll never come back. I won't ever see you again."

"I've got to go back and arrange things for Louise. I'll take her away this summer and in the fall I'll have Hammond find something for me out here."

"What about the picture now," she asked, "won't you come back to finish it?"

"Henry won't be able to wait. My plans will be too indefinite."

"But it's your story," she protested.

"Luke Rodgers will probably do it. He and Henry have done some good things together."

"I can't believe that I'm never going to see you again," she said.

"Don't say that," he said, "we'll be together again. It's just that I don't know exactly when."

"I know now that you love her," Alma said. "You're tied to her because of this dreadful thing. You think it separated you. It didn't really. It didn't at all. It's bound you to her."

"You're wrong, Alma. But I just can't leave her now, how the hell can I?"

"I understand," she said, "really I do, Gordon, it's just that I've never loved anyone before but you, and now you're going away . . ." she twisted the ends of her belt.

He went to her and held her.

"Never anyone but you," she said, "you know that. I used to think there was something the matter with me."

"My baby," he said, "there's nothing the matter with you. You're the most exciting woman I ever knew."

"Only with you," she clung to him. "Only with you, I tried with others and it didn't work. I hated it. They thought I was cold, even the doctor."

"Baby, baby, we know that isn't true." He kissed her to stop her trembling.

She raised her head and looked at him the way she had earlier in the patio.

"Gordon," she said, "for the last time, for good-bye."

He felt the small, sharp bones at her hips move against him.

He covered them with his hands and held her still. "Not good-bye," he said, "not the last time."

"Now," she said, whispering, "now."

"It won't make it any easier, baby."

"Now . . ."

He looked at her for a long moment, then went to the door and locked it.

CHAPTER THIRTEEN *S*H E awakened, sitting
bolt upright, her fingers twisting the edge of the sheet.
When she realized where she was, she dropped back on
the bed and rolled her head from side to side. It was
Gordon who was, by now, on the plane, yet Gordon had
not been in her dream. She tried to remember the
dream, to put it together. She had been with Ray flying
from New York to Los Angeles, it was (in the dream)
just after they had been married. There was a storm
and she had been afraid and her fear of the storm mixed
with the gnawing, shaming fear of what would happen
now that Ray was her husband. Ray's hand had rested
passively yet possessively on her arm, trying to quiet her,
but it had given her a kind of panic. "I can't. I won't.
I'll say that I'm ill, or too tired. I won't. I can't."

But that was long ago. Everything was changed now
because of Gordon. He had changed everything, he had
changed her. Would it not have been better if he'd
never seen her, never touched her, never made her as

other women, because now she was in great pain, the tearing pain of flesh parted from beloved flesh. It was not the unhappiness that she had known when she faced the failure of her marriage to Ray. This was an animal pain and, like an animal, she wanted to be left alone with it. She didn't want the comfort and succor and kind words of people. All she wanted was Gordon and she couldn't have him, ever. It might well kill her, she thought, it was killing her now.

For a while after he had left she had locked herself in her room and she had fallen into a torpid state. The pain had subsided; it was as if she had administered an anaesthetic to herself, which, though feeling nothing now, she knew would wear off and the hurt return.

And now it was wearing off and she must begin the first of the nights without him. This would have been the time for his call. Tonight there would be no call. Tonight she would not bathe and dress and do her hair for him, because he would not be here.

Her face felt sore from rubbing against his cheek. She had bit his lip, bit it until it bled.

Like animals gnawing at each other. She felt shame. He had done this to her, made her capable of such behavior, Alma Fletcher, the prettiest, daintiest girl in Kensington, biting a man's lip, allowing him to do things that the other girls had whispered about, flushed and wide-eyed in the contagion of their excitement and ignorance. She'd said, "Don't be disgusting!" to those other girls years ago. And now she was the same, no she was worse, she had done things they'd never even dreamed of in those high-school days. She had sinned, sinned. She was defiled, degraded, doing things like that

192

with a man. It was indecent, nice girls, well brought up girls, didn't, wouldn't. And with a married man, when she wouldn't have let Ray Tavis when she was married to him and a man whose child had died only a few hours before. It made it worse than indecent.

She jumped out of bed and ran to the bathroom and retched horribly.

But she couldn't throw up and after a while, still feeling sick, she half-crawled back to bed. She couldn't seem to stand up straight. Her mother had been so proud of her posture and so had the gym teacher, Miss Ryerson. "Alma's beautiful carriage," they'd called it. Miss Ryerson had told her things too, advised her. "Can't be too careful, a girl who looks as you do, Alma, and well, boys will take liberties, you mustn't allow it. You're too lovely, oh much too lovely," and Miss Ryerson had leaned forward and kissed her cheek. Her lips had been hairy and she'd smelled of mint. "And Alma," she'd said, "I don't think you should wear that kind of bra . . . well, it might give them some ideas, don't you think?"

"I must be vile," she said to herself. "It wasn't Gordon's fault. I made him do it, rubbing against him, begging him. For the last time, I said, for good-bye . . . And he'd told me about that poor little creature. That must have been like Mrs. Young's grandchild, the one we used to see in her yard, drooling and cooing. I wonder how he died. I never even asked Gordon that."

There was a slight sound at the door.

"Mrs. Tavis, can I fix you something?"

"Nothing, Ivy."

"Won't you just let me come in and straighten the room? I'll only take a minute, Mrs. Tavis."

"No, please."

"Mrs. Calder is very anxious for you to phone her. She keeps calling."

"All right."

"Will you speak if she calls again?"

"Tell her I'm resting. You go on home, Ivy."

Sue was probably all upset but she was the last person Alma wanted to see. "I don't want to see anyone, I want them all to leave me alone."

Sue was lucky, Sue was safe and Sue was good. And I am not good, Alma said, *Oh, forgive me. Forgive me.* She did not know to whom she was appealing. To her God, she supposed, her Sunday School God, but He seemed terribly far away and uncaring.

Ivy came to the door again and tried the knob gently and gently called, but Alma didn't answer.

2

Fasten your seat belts. That meant rough weather ahead, Gordon thought, although at the moment the plane was perfectly steady. He fastened the wide webbing bands loosely around his waist and picked up the copy of *Time* he had been reading. The plane lurched, righted itself, dipped and lurched again. Gordon looked out of the small window but saw only thick, white clouds clotted and cottony far below.

He lowered his chair a little and, slipping the magazine in the pocket in front of him, closed his eyes.

194

What was below the clouds, he wondered? No longer Southern California. As they had flown out over Los Angeles he thought, *I'll never see it again*. He'd had that same thought since morning about everything: emptying the drawers in his room at the Bel Vista, walking down the long bare corridor to Henry's office, past the water cooler, past the reception room, to the door with Henry's name on its neat brass plate. Writers' doors had only typewritten cards that could be slipped in and out. Quick mortality. He knew that tomorrow the white card with GORDON CRAM on it would be removed. Maybe Marge would do it, nice, bright, efficient Marge, the best secretary he'd ever had—he must remember to send her something at Christmas.

And Sue, he should have telephoned Sue to say good-bye. It might have softened the censure she'd had for him. At dinner two nights ago she'd said, "It isn't what separates people that interests me, it's what keeps them together."

Now she would discuss it with Alma, mull over it. They'd analyze it, dissect it, worry it endlessly. *Well let them*, he thought. It was not a secret any longer, it was not anything.

Again he had the sense that he was not measuring time properly. Could it have been only last night that he had told Alma that he loved her? Alma, in her black dress, across the table from him and leaving the restaurant, going home together and the long, lovely night afterwards. Alma had told him today that he loved Louise. *Well*, he thought, shifting in his seat, *I never said I didn't love Louise*.

Alma, what was she doing now? Probably with Sue

195

Calder at this moment and already beginning to hate him. With his tongue he touched the swollen blue bruise on his lower lip.

The plane was rising until the piece of sky that Gordon saw through its window was the strong blue of carbon paper. California was far behind and as far removed from him, already as much a part of the past as Carthage. It lay behind him abandoned, razed to the ground, sown with salt. His own wasteland.

Hollywood, Carthage. Carthage and Hollywood. He had read something, somewhere years ago, it was in the back of his mind, that linked the two names in his thought. "I'll ask Louise, she'll remember. She always remembers things like that. Something about to Carthage then I came. Louise will know."

He unfastened the seat belt as the sign went off. He drew the little curtain at the window, stretched his legs and made himself as comfortable as he could. After a while he slept.

CHAPTER FOURTEEN G O R D O N waited at the corner of Fifth Avenue and Fifty-eighth Street for the traffic light to change. The April sunlight was warm and strong, like the sun of summer rather than early spring.

He looked at his watch. Sue had been emphatic that he should not be late.

Might as well go there now, Gordon said to himself, walking toward the Plaza.

He had not seen the Calders for a year. Would he be the first or would they? For the first few minutes it would be awkward and uneasy. There would be, he imagined, some strain and strangeness after what had happened.

The city is the place to be in the spring, Gordon thought. Last year at this time, as he would never forget, he had been in Hollywood. He crossed the street thinking that in a city spring showed itself in small, swift flashes. One day there a sudden outcropping of awnings on the fronts of apartment houses, another day flower carts would appear in the streets filled with earthen pots of geranium and bunches of yellow and white flowers with spring-sounding names, jonquil and daffodil and narcissus.

He observed that the sun, glancing off the side of a building, turned a high row of windows into sun-struck mirrors; children held balloons on thin sticks, little boys wore sailor suits and blew on brand-new whistles; the delicate city trees showed evidence of feathery green leaf. Each small sign of spring in the city seemed to be significant, to have another enigmatic reason, while in the country, Gordon mused, there was nothing the least secret about it, it was blatant, the ponderous turning of the earth, nature heavily underscoring another season.

Or perhaps I just hate the country, Gordon thought, stopping at a shop window to look at a display of wrist watches. People, he then noticed, were staring up at the sky and he did the same. A tiny plane was twirling and spinning at a great height, issuing a slender stream of white vapor and spelling out with it the name and merits of a bottled drink.

Gordon watched for a moment, amused. It added to his pleasure in the day, in the city. He liked Saturdays, a left-over from childhood, he supposed and he hated not to have something special to do on Saturday.

He walked to the windows of Bergdorf-Goodman and inspected the navy-blue polka-dot dress on a frozen wax mannequin. It was a pretty dress with full skirt and a wide belt. *If I had a girl,* thought Gordon, idly and not unhappily, *I'd go in and buy that dress for her.* It would look fine on a long-legged girl walking along Fifth

Avenue. Across the street on the other side of the Plaza stood four vestigial, romantic horse cabs. Two children and an elderly woman were climbing into one of them. *If I had a girl,* Gordon continued his thought, *I'd buy her the dotted dress and we'd ride through the park in a cab. Then I'd take her to lunch. This is the kind of a day to lunch with a girl, rather than with the Calders.*

Sue had said that they would be at the Fifty-ninth Street side but he went up the steps of the Fifth Avenue entrance. He walked around, past the palms, past the newsstand, glancing as he invariably did at the new magazines, and then he saw them.

They were not alone, as he had expected. Two men were with them and a woman. Her back was to Gordon but there was something about the way she was standing, that elegant, arrogant posture—could it be, from here it looked like—Alma?

He stopped for a second, feeling the way he once had when he'd opened a door in a house that was unfamiliar to him and had nearly fallen down a steep flight of steps. Then he looked again.

They were talking and didn't see him. He had the impulse to leave. He'd telephone and say he couldn't make it.

At that second Sue saw him and waved a white-gloved hand. He walked on toward them.

"Gordon," she said, and kissed him.

"Hello, Susie. This is nice."

Sue slipped an arm through his; the other woman turned around. "You're late, I've been waiting to see you," she said.

199

It was not Alma. It was Jean Fielding and she was looking handsome in black.

"Take off the sun glasses," he said, "it can't have been that bad a night."

Jean took off the glasses and gave him her hand and the smile.

I forgot about the smile, Gordon thought, shaking hands with Henry. He was introduced to the two men. One was Harry Durand, an agent, the other a man called Joe. Gordon didn't hear his last name.

"Let's go," Harry Durand said to Joe.

"Wait a minute, boys," Jean said, "you can drop me at Twenty One."

"Won't you lunch with us, Jeanie?" Henry Calder asked.

"Can't. Love to, but can't. I have to meet some woman who writes a column in the Asbury Park *News*. The studio really fixes me when I get to New York."

"Why not skip it?" Henry said.

"If you must be going . . ." Sue said.

"Henry, my honey, see you," Jean said, then she looked at Gordon. "Hear you're writing a play."

"That is the rumor," he said.

"Is there a part for me?"

"I don't know," Gordon said, "I've only read the first act."

"Call me at the Pierre," she said, twirling the sun glasses. "I'll be in town for a few weeks. Let's have a drink and talk about everything. The Pierre."

Gordon nodded.

She put on her glasses. " 'Bye," she said.

"Good-bye," they all said. Every head in the lobby turned to watch her go.

"Well, Calders," Gordon said, taking each by the arm, "you're a fine sight. Susie, with that hat you look like a New York girl."

"Let's have a drink," Henry proposed, "to celebrate our reunion."

They sat at a round table in the Oak Room and looked across at Central Park.

"I love this hotel," Sue said, "why don't we ever stay here?"

"I did once," Henry answered, "before we were married. With Ray Tavis. He always stays here."

"I remember," Sue said involuntarily.

Henry looked uncomfortable.

"It's all right, kids," Gordon said, "the name can be mentioned in my presence."

"What about the drink before we get down to talking?" Henry said.

"I think it's a martini day," Sue suggested, "a terribly, terribly dry martini day."

"Three martinis," Gordon ordered, "dry."

"Now tell me the news," Gordon asked, "how are the small Calders?"

"Fine, and it's lovely to be away from them," Sue said. "Are you really writing a play?"

"I'm writing something. I hope it turns out to be a play."

"Apparently so does Miss Fielding," said Sue.

"When I came in," Gordon said, "there was something about her—for a second I thought it was Alma."

"They don't look a bit alike," Sue said.

"I know what you mean," Henry said, "that calculated stance of the professional beauty."

"How is Alma?" Gordon asked as the drinks came to the table.

"She's all right," Sue said. "She went to Sun Valley for a month with the Altmans. The change was good for her."

There was a pause.

"She sent me a post card from there," Gordon said, "I'm glad she's well."

"Well, I wouldn't exactly rave over her condition," Sue said, "but she's better."

"She should go to work," Henry said.

"There really isn't much for her to do," Sue pointed out.

"There's always baskets to the poor, or china painting," Henry said.

"She was offered a job on *Vogue*. Nail-polish editor or something like that."

"Here in New York?" Gordon asked.

"No, in Hollywood. She doesn't want to come to New York. We asked her to come along with us but she wouldn't."

"It's a big town," Gordon said.

"It's not only you," Sue said.

"Let's have another drink."

"Where is Tavis?" Gordon asked, after he had ordered the drinks.

"Making a picture in Paris. He called Alma and asked her to come over."

Gordon looked startled.

"I wouldn't be surprised if he still had a sneaker for her," Henry added.

"But she wouldn't go back to him, would she?"

"I think it's quite possible," Henry said. "Let's have a look at the menu."

2

THEY parted at the end of lunch after making plans to have dinner and go to the theater together on the following Wednesday night.

"How did you think he looked?" Henry asked Sue when they were alone.

"The way he always has looked," Sue said. "Gordon has hardly changed at all since I've known him. He has a well developed sense of self-preservation."

"What's that got to do with it?"

"Look at how Alma has changed. I don't believe the thing touched Gordon a bit."

"I think you're wrong. It touched him a lot. He was crazy about Alma, but as things worked out he had to stay with Louise."

"Perhaps," Sue said. "But there just aren't big romances any more, are there? It's the wrong century for them. Everything is so temperate and controlled between people. Love affairs don't have *size* the way they used to, even in our grandparents' time. Everything is so open and uninhibited now, nothing clandestine and mortal any more. No wild elopements or duels or women taking to nunneries. People get married and divorced and married again, all very friendly and the burning need for the person one loves vanishes. Passion has become—casual!"

"What brought all this on?" Henry demanded, "just because Alma sent Gordon a post card from Sun Valley."

"A *post card!*" Sue said, shaking her head. "From a woman who said that she couldn't live without him."

"Better that way," Henry said. "It may not conform with your ideas about life and love but it's a lot easier on the nervous system."

"Funny," Sue said, "that that's all it comes down to, the end of the grand passion, drop me a line, take care of your cold, that's all that's left."

"Don't worry about it," Henry said, "I'm crazy about you and I'll prove it. Let's go over to Schwartz's and see if there are any new toys for the kids."

3

GORDON watched the Calders walk down the street with a feeling of affection. How nice that they didn't change, what a durable and rewarding thing their marriage was! *Mustn't forget Wednesday night,* he thought, *I'll get the tickets Monday. Hope Louise won't be difficult about going. She never liked Sue.*

He walked through Central Park still thinking of what Henry had said about Alma returning to Ray Tavis. At first it sounded fantastic but, as he thought about it, he saw reasons for it. Alma was still unready for other men, she had retreated to that marble cool-ness in which he had found her and, perhaps due to the circumstances of their relation, she'd never emerge again, because that meant a giving and she would have learned that there is pain as well as happiness contained in such love. But at least with Ray they both knew what they were getting, they understood the other and they were both older and, it could be assumed, wiser. They would probably work out a fairly good life for themselves and Alma would not be alone. *Anyway*, Gordon thought, *she'll never find another man quite as concerned with what she should wear.*

But it startled him that his meditations gave him a queer feeling in the stomach. He hadn't seen her for a year, or heard a word from her except that post card. But you can't have been in love with someone and not have something left, a residue of emotion, of memory and desire. "And in April too!" Gordon thought, smiling a little, "the cruelest month."

No, he would not forget Alma, even though it was over between them entirely. She had known it would be when he came to tell her that he had to go to New York. No doubt he had known, too.

Children roller-skated past him as he walked and nurses wheeled babies in carriages. He saw old men shifting their bones on the benches to follow the descent of the sun in the sky.

He looked at them and he saw Alma. He heard the boys playing baseball, and in his ears there was the sound of her voice.

He had reached the reservoir by now and he decided to walk around it, something he hadn't done for months.

His thoughts remained with Alma. Last year at this time he'd returned to New York and to Louise, who, in the doctor's words, was in a state of agitated depression.

As soon as she was well enough they had flown to Europe and spent the summer there. A surprisingly agreeable summer. In August, Louise had said she would love to go to Venice but to Gordon this seemed impossible, with its new connotation as the place he had wanted to take Alma. He had persuaded Louise to go to Lake Como instead.

Just before they had left for Europe he had sent Alma a telegram. He had been with Louise almost constantly, so there had been no chance to telephone or even write. The telegram had seemed aseptic and impersonal to him even though he had written it over and over trying to make it as intimate as possible.

Soon after they returned from Europe in September Louise went to Chicago over a week end to represent Dover House at a booksellers' convention. That Friday night Gordon had done what he later supposed he'd been planning to do all summer. After dinner alone he had started to clear out his file when, without any conscious forethought, he went to the telephone and asked to speak person to person to Mrs. Tavis at Crestview 6-8101 in Beverly Hills.

Then there was suddenly her voice, just as he remembered it, answering the telephone.

"This *is* Mrs. Tavis," she'd said.

"Hello, Alma."

"Oh! Oh!" the voice wavered, then recovered, "where are you?"

"In New York. I just wanted to find out how you are."

"Oh, I see," she said, her voice still shaky with surprise. "When did you get back from Europe?"

"Tuesday. This is the first chance I had to call."

"Was it a good summer? Did you write a lot?"

"It was interesting," he said.

So they had talked but, like most telephone conversations, it was limited and frustrating and unsatisfactory but better than nothing, better than silence.

"What are you doing?" he asked. "Are you in your room?"

"Yes, at the desk. I'm not doing anything, just going over bills and things."

It had been easy for him to imagine her in the pale-green room that he knew so well. "What have you got on?"

"A gray skirt," she said, "and a white linen blouse you've never seen."

"Have you had dinner yet?"

"No, I'm going to now and then to the movies with Peggy Duncan, remember her? She's alone. Bobby's on location. She's going to have a baby."

"Certainly I remember her, we met her at the Calders'. Are you all right?"

She told him that she'd been ill and that her sister Roselle had come to stay with her. They'd flown to Mexico for a week.

Now she was planning to go to Sun Valley with the Altmans for a month and learn to ski.

"That sounds like fun," he said, "but don't break one of those beautiful legs."

Then there was one of those silences more telling than talk.

"Well, I just wanted to know how you were," he said rather lamely.

"Thank you," she said, "I'm fine, Gordon. Thank you for calling me."

He felt the sadness and the lostness and the aloneness through everything she had said and it tore at him with the ineffectual claws of pity. There seemed no reason to prolong the conversation. "Good night, Alma," he said softly.

"Gordon, don't hang up!" there was a note of urgency in her voice.

"All right," he said, "I don't want to either—it's just so hopeless. Maybe I shouldn't have called. Maybe I should have left you alone."

"No, this is wonderful," she protested, "talk more, it's so good to hear you. It's been so long."

But they really didn't have much to say to each other. They'd been lovers, but they hadn't had time to become friends or loved long enough to be enemies. There was nothing left for them to be to each other.

"Good-bye, Gordon."

"Good-bye, Alma."

He was heavy-hearted as he hung up. Then he sat in the living room thinking about their brief, incisive past, remembering times when they had been together more sharply than he had allowed himself to since he left Hollywood.

But the telephone call was unsatisfactory. Nothing had been gained. Gordon decided not to repeat it. Louise returned from Chicago and he went to the station to meet her. She was embarrassingly happy at this unexpected attention.

So that was that, he thought, looking at the pale slapping water of the reservoir. He and Louise were to-

208

gether, and she was happier than she had been in years. As for Alma, sometimes the idea of that beauty and love and warmth being wasted, day after day, distressed him. But Alma was not his problem as Louise was, as living the rest of his life was. Life had imposed a responsibility on him that was greater than his desire or happiness. He didn't even think this articulately; he merely accepted it as Alma had known it intuitively the day he'd told her the whole story of himself and Louise. And now that story was over or at least the turbulent part of it. They were married, he and Louise, and they would stay married, he thought, for as long as they lived.

He deliberately turned his attention to the play and started to figure out a curtain for the second act.

It was nearly 4:30 before he found himself back, hardly knowing it, at the Fifty-ninth Street entrance of the Park. There was a new chill in the air as evening approached.

"I could go home," he considered, "or stop in to see the Braque show at the gallery or go to a newsreel." But, then, as he had known he was going to, he looked across the street at the Hotel Pierre.

He crossed Fifth Avenue, went into the lobby and found a public telephone booth. He deposited a nickel and dialed his own number. Louise answered.

"When did you get in, Loulie?"

"About ten minutes ago."

"I've been trying to get you all afternoon," he said. "Something has come up with Henry and I may be stuck for a while."

"Oh, I see," she said.

"If I'm not home by six," he said, "go along to Mary's

without me. I'll be there as soon as I can. What's the address again?"

"121 East Twelfth Street," Louise said, "don't disappoint her."

"Of course not," he said, "I'll be there. Good-bye, honey—you understand?"

"Of course, but come as soon as you can. I promised to help Mary or I'd wait here for you."

"I know," he said, "see you later."

Then he looked up the number of the Pierre in the directory, deposited another nickel, dialed the number and asked for Miss Jean Fielding.

"Who is calling?" It was Jean's voice.

"Mr. Cram."

"Gordon?"

"You sound surprised," he said, thinking of the smile.

"Yes, I am."

"I've been reading the second act. I think there is a part for you."

"I'd love to hear about it," she said, "when can you come over?"

"Now."

"I have some people here. Where are you?"

"Downstairs."

She laughed. "Give me ten minutes," she said, "then come up. 1121 and 1122."

"One room will be enough," he said.

"What do you want to drink?"

"Scotch old-fashioned."

"What do you need for that?"

"Scotch," he said.

"You've got it," she said.

He opened the door of the booth and passed through the lobby onto the street. The day had darkened; in the intense spring sky there was a pale flickering of the first stars. From the park the breeze carried the scent of turned earth and mixed it with the acrid smells of the city. He breathed deeply, watching the lights go on in the windows high above him.

He glanced at his watch. "I'll walk around the block," he said to himself, "that will be about it."

Smiling, he joined the moving crowds on Madison Avenue and caught their own quick pace.

This was the hour that he loved most in the city, the hour that seemed to promise so much. There was something nostalgic and a little sad in the early evening air. But tonight there was something expectant as well.